TOO LITTLE . . .

Chiun. Through his kaleidoscopic vision, Remo saw him, lying like a statue on the stone floor. He reached out his hand to touch him. The old man was cold.

"Chiun," Remo whispered unbelievingly. He couldn't be dead. He couldn't be.

The anger that rose in him turned to hatred, and the hatred brought him to his feet. The hatred electrified his useless shoulder and forced his arm back and ahead, into the throat of one of the guards, as his left hand exploded into the skull of another. There was no pain, because the hatred was stronger than the pain. He kicked a third guard in the groin, sending him flying in a screaming heap. He held another by the hair as he bashed the guard's head into the stone floor.

Then Remo saw the brass staff swinging prettily through the air an inch from his face, and it was too late. Randy Nooner's face was twisted into an ugly mask, her teeth bared, as she brought the staff down. Remo ducked his head. It was all he could do.

And he thought sadly, as the pain of the blow registered and the blackness began to envelop him, that he had failed. He would never see Chiun again.

. . . TOO LATE

The Destroyer #45

SPOILS OF WAR

Warren Murphy

PINNACLE BOOKS   NEW YORK

DESTROYER #45: SPOILS OF WAR

Copyright © 1981 by Richard Sapir and Warren Murphy

An original Pinnacle Books edition, published for the first time anywhere.

First printing, August 1981

ISBN: 0-523-40719-X

Cover illustration by Hector Garrido

Printed in the United States of America

PINNACLE BOOKS, INC.
1430 Broadway
New York, New York 10018

For Margaret Richardson McBride,
with love and appreciation, and for the
Glorious House of Sinanju, P.O. Box 1454,
Secaucus, NJ 07094

SPOILS OF WAR

One

On the day he pushed the man off the Pontusket Bridge, Artemis Thwill knew he was free. More than free. He was launched. He hadn't expected to kill the man, or even start to push, even though he had often thought such things. He would be standing near a curb watching a woman balance two heavy packages and wonder what it would look like if he threw a body block into her lower spine. Artemis weighed 228 pounds. He was six feet, two inches tall and had played linebacker for Iowa State.

He was a senior vice-president for Inter-Agro-Chem. So Artemis Thwill did not go around throwing blocks into ladies with packages. He went around offering to help carry packages, joining the Congregational Church, and coaching in the Pee Wee League.

But he would see the little boys with their big expensive shoulder pads and their little twigs of neck between the two and imagine himself roaring onto the field yelling, "Let's have some real hitting, you little spoiled-ass bastards!"

Then he would see himself smash a fist into one

1

of the wobbly helmets on the twig necks and collapse a kid with a satisfying thwump. Then he would take a pair of little ankles with his fingers and use his 67-pound offensive tackle as a swinging club and go through his lineup screaming that this was where he was separating the men from the boys, as he separated a birdlike ten-year-old arm from its shoulder joint.

All this he imagined. He even imagined the parents staring horrified at the crushed bodies lying around the Pee Wee League field. And he would say, "They never would have made real football players. Get this shit off my field."

That was the scene that played in his head as he wrote a lengthy report on how football was physically and emotionally unhealthy for the children, and formed a parents' league for sane athletics.

He was called on often to talk around the country, and he had a very good speech to do it. He would even choke and sometimes cry when he would tell parents in Duluth or Yonkers, "You take these twigs of necks between those bulky plastic helmets and those shoulder pads, and my God, I can see them snap. What would happen—just imagine what would happen—if you slammed your own fist into one of those helmets. It would be like a pinball game."

It was also good business for Inter-Agro-Chem. It made publicity. And since Inter-Agro-Chem had been accused of poisoning more river beds than Hitler did minds, it wanted to appear sensitive to people's needs. Coming out against tackle football for tykes made Inter-Agro-Chem look good. Especially when this was done by one of their senior vice-presidents—Iowa State '60, Harvard Business School '62, Artemis Thwill.

That's what Artemis Thwill had done with his desire to pulverize little necks. At one of his community talks, a man rose who had remembered Artemis Thwill from Pontusket High School. He remembered that Artemis hadn't had a pair of pants without a patch on them until he started playing football. He remembered that no Thwill in Pontusket had ever even owned a house larger than a used mobile home, until Artemis started playing football. He pointed out that Artemis had earned an education through football and enough money playing second string for a professional club to go to graduate school and that without football, Artemis might presently be spreading fertilizer instead of directing people who manufactured it, directing people from a big desk in a big office with a pretty secretary and a traveling expense account of $22,800.

To this man Artemis Thwill answered softly, breathing into his voice the outrage of most of the people whom he knew were on his side. Like most meetings anywhere, people came to hear what they wanted to hear from people who wanted them to believe what they already believed. This was called by various names: consciousness raising, proseletyzing, or telling it like it is. Artemis had the crowd.

"It's true I was poor," said Artemis. And the people, his people, growled slightly, their outrage fueled.

"It's true I didn't have a pair of pants without a patch," said Artemis. "But I ask you, what sort of a system makes young boys hit other boys in order to get an education."

Applause. He knew this crowd thought all the ills

of the world were brought on by this recent civilization, which had in reality made more progress in the last half-century than all mankind did in its first million centuries. The pro football crowd, on the other hand, thought all the ills of the world were brought on by these people.

In other words, everyone was talking cow droppings, and six foot, two inches tall Artemis Thwill, with the blond hair receding just slightly, and the soft blue eyes and massive shoulders and stern chin, knew how to out-drop any Guernsey this side of a Pontusket pasture.

"Maybe if we taught with kindness and enlightenment instead of fear, maybe, just maybe, we wouldn't have people who felt a need to kill other people," Artemis said softly, with full knowledge that his nation's streets had become unsafe in direct proportion to all the understanding and kindness forced on its police departments.

That was what Artemis had said. What he imagined doing was punching the man in the penis with a 228-pound uppercut. He imagined saying, "You're right. I am white trash and this is how I settle things."

That was what Artemis wanted to do.

But not until Artemis threw the man off the bridge did he ever do what he wanted to do.

That day was March and bitter, and the fields were wet with melted ice and snow and the rivers beginning to gorge. The man was watching the ice break and flow.

"Don't jump," yelled Artemis, running from his car.

"Don't jump," yelled Artemis, pushing the man up the railing.

4

"Don't jump," yelled Artemis, smashing the man's clinging hands until they let go.

"Oh, my God, help," yelled the man.

"Crazy fool," yelled Artemis. "You had so much to live for."

The man hit ice below like a garbage bag full of gravel. You could hear the head crack solid against the ice floe, and then the body went splash and the man went flowing downriver, wedged beneath the ice.

Only for a moment did Artemis Thwill regret what he had done. This was not a high enough bridge to be absolutely sure the man was dead. Next time it would have to be a certain death. For Artemis Thwill knew, even before the man hit the water, that he would do this again.

Thwill knew what made him such a good football player back in college. He liked to hurt. But most of all, he discovered on this chill delicious March day, he loved to kill.

There was of course an investigation. Artemis told the police he really didn't want too much recognition for trying to save the man's life. He thought it might disturb an already disturbed widow. "If only we had more psychiatric counseling," said Artemis Thwill.

"The wife says he didn't commit suicide," said the Pontusket chief of police, who did not believe in psychiatric counseling, and felt himself a hypocrite for not announcing that the police department ought only to protect people from other people, not people from themselves.

"Poor thing," said Artemis.

"She says he always went to that bridge to walk," said the chief.

5

"Poor thing," said Artemis.

"She says she thinks you threw him over, Mr. Thwill."

"Poor thing," said Artemis.

"Did you?"

"Of course," said Artemis with the chill cutting edge of one of the town leaders to one of the town servants.

"Sorry, I had to ask, Mr. Thwill."

"That's all right," said Artemis, with deep understanding in his voice. Artemis knew understanding properly used could be more insulting and humiliating than spit in the face. "Perhaps I ought to speak to the woman."

"She's pretty upset, Mr. Thwill. She don't think he rightly did do himself in, considering he ordered a new pickup truck for tomorrow."

"I understand," said Artemis. The man owned a small farm, which he helped support with his fulltime job at the feed grain store. He had been 35. His wife was 22. They were childless.

She sat in the kitchen of their small house, her hands cracked and red from kneading. Her lips were drawn tight and white. She had melon breasts. She stared hatred at Artemis Thwill as he entered. She did not get up. The police chief introduced Artemis.

Artemis said how truly sorrowful he was. Artemis thought how he'd like to put his hands on the rose print dress, specifically around the breasts.

"You killed him, you son of a bitch, you bastard," screamed the woman.

The police chief, embarrassed, turned his head away. Artemis quickly grabbed a breast. The woman said nothing. Artemis removed the hand before the chief turned back.

6

"You poor thing," said Artemis.

"Killed him, you bastard. Thoughtless son of a bitch. Thoughtless."

"I'm sorry you feel that way," rumbled Artemis, his eyes fixated on her heaving bosom.

"How the hell am I supposed to feel? Insurance policies never pay off for suicides."

It was then, in that small farmhouse, that Artemis Thwill fell in love. Here was a woman raised in the country, probably not even a graduate of high school, with all the wisdom and understanding of a Harvard Graduate School of Business alumna.

Her name was Samantha, and Artemis stayed for dinner when the chief left. He learned you didn't need a master's degree to learn reason. You didn't have to run a country to show understanding. Truly and for the first time, Artemis Thwill had found a woman with whom he could share his life.

"You could have hit him on the head, simple as that, and left him there. Why'd you have to throw him over to make it look like a suicide? Sheesh."

"I didn't think," Artemis said, filled with remorse. His cashmere coat seemed out of place in the rustic kitchen. He knew he had to give Samantha better than this.

"Well, you should have."

"I can't change my story now."

"Why'd you do it in the first place?"

Artemis thought. He pondered the atavistic rage that prompted people to kill, and the warped social structure that took normal, home-loving persons and drove them to snuff out the lives of innocents. "I felt like it," Artemis said.

"Best damned reason for doing anything," said Samantha.

They made love that instant, and the next day Artemis did not return to his home. In the ensuing week he learned much wisdom from the young farm girl.

"Look, our only chance long range is if God does not exist," Samantha said. " 'Cause if he does, we've had it. And don't give me this repentance crap, cause God don't take too many and even if we did repent, we'd be liars."

"How can you say that, Samantha?" Artemis crooned.

"Bejeezus, I love it when you're hypocritical. Just love it. You're so good at it. With your hypocrisy and my brains, we can do anything." And for the next few days, Samantha thought, deeply, carefully. The only words she uttered during those days were, "I think I've got it. I think I've got it."

On the third day, with the sun setting red over the straw and mud fields of Iowa, Samantha shrieked to wake the dead. "That's it!" yelled Samantha.

"What? What?" Artemis asked.

"I've got it. It's the only business that lasts. In it, you can do anything you want. Hell, your victims will have to figure out what they did wrong to deserve it."

"What is it?"

"And hypocrisy?" She laughed, high and clear as a bell. "You can cripple your victims and then tell them you're the purest soul ever walked the earth, and make 'em believe it. Make them feel like dilly poo if they don't."

"Whaaat?" yelled Artemis, shaking Samantha's shoulders.

"Artemis. You're perfect for it." She planted a big

8

wet kiss on his lips. "Artie, honey, you're going into the God business."

Artemis Thwill's hand rose involuntarily to his throat. "You mean be a preacher?" he said, aghast. "Me? Give up my senior vice-presidency to become a fifteen-thousand-dollar-a-year Holy Roller?"

"No," Samantha said sweetly. "To become God."

Two

His name was Remo and he was flying like a captive god.

The dragon's skin felt pebbled under his fingertips. Remo held on tight as the giant fire-breathing beast soared through the air, trailing Remo behind like some other-worldly water skier. The clouds below him billowed plump and white.

Remo coiled himself into a tight ball to bring his body closer to the dragon's. Once near enough, he would work a multiple attack in a fast inside line on the beast's underside, turning as he worked to cover space while still maintaining a grip on the tether. It was a modification of an attack taught to him years before by the Master of Sinanju.

But the Master had taught him only the secrets for assassinating men, not dragons. Chiun, the Master, had explained to Remo that man was the only species capable of producing specimens dangerous enough to require extermination. Any animal, Chiun claimed, would lose its desire to kill if offered food, or the return of its young, or its proper territory where it could live in peace, or the cessation of physical torment. Not man. Man would kill

10

for greed, for power, or for fun. Man could kill and destroy and pervert and return to do it all again. Of all the life forms on earth, Chiun said, only man could wreak destruction on life itself.

Only man, if you didn't count the monster that was carrying Remo toward certain death.

Remo's attack hadn't even altered the course of the dragon's flight. Its skin was heavier than tank armor. The beast was the size of three square city blocks. It headed with deafening speed toward the blackness of space, where even Remo, with a nervous system developed far beyond the capacity of normal men, would die helpless and gasping.

He made one last attempt. Grateful for the years of exercises under Chiun's tutelage, he spun in a rapid series of six somersaults, which propelled him more than 20 stories high—high enough to land on the dragon's back. If he could land safely on the beast, he could crawl up to the animal's slender neck and find a vulnerable spot. . . .

He did not land. While he was still in midair on the crest of his last somersault, the dragon turned sharply and faced Remo with its glowing eyes. The sight was paralyzing. Remo's hands fell from the thin tether, his only connection to life. And as he began to fall, the beast opened its maw and spewed fire onto Remo's plummeting form, setting it aflame and speaking in a voice that came from another universe:

"It is the legend, come now to fruition."

"Chiun!" Remo screamed. "Master, my father!"

And suddenly the flames that charred his body were extinguished, and his fall had been gently broken, and his forehead felt cool and damp. "Awake, my son," said a high, squeaky, familiar voice.

Remo sat up abruptly in bed. "I was dreaming, Chiun."

The old Oriental nodded. He was wearing a shimmering purple robe pulled loosely across his tiny, frail-looking frame. His white beard and mustache rested like snow against the vibrant purple of the robe. On his head he wore a squat coolie's hat.

"What are you dressed like that for?" Remo asked, trying to force his senses to clarity. He wasn't used to sleeping. He felt drugged.

"The Master of Sinanju clothes himself as he wishes," Chiun said.

Remo stood up, wobbling, and rubbed his face with his hands, feeling the thin line of sweat at his hairline and on his upper lip. Incredulously, he stared at his hands.

Remo did not sweat. The years of training in the ways of Sinanju had given him the tools of the finest assassin on earth, but they had exacted their price in other ways. The body-wracking discipline of Sinanju had gradually evolved his nervous system into that of another being, far more highly developed than even the strongest or fastest normal man, so that, for all the things Remo could do, he did not sweat. And he did not sleep, not the sprawled-out, dream-laden sleep of regular human beings. Yet he had slept, and he had dreamed, and he was sweating.

"How long was I out?" he asked.

"Seven hours."

Remo panicked. He hadn't slept seven hours straight in more than ten years. He felt sweat trickling down his chest and back. His head throbbed with a dull pain. "What's happening to me?" he asked quietly. "What's wrong?"

"Nothing is wrong, my son." The aged Oriental tucked his long-nailed hands into the sleeves of his kimono. "The Dream of Death is a natural process for those trained in the mysteries of Sinanju. It is a coming of age. Now is your time."

Chiun floated to the tatami mat on the floor, where he arranged himself in the elaborate folds of his robe. His face broke into a broad grin. "To cheer you, I will share with you a legend of the glory that is Sinanju," he said magnanimously. "It is known throughout Korea."

"Oh, no," Remo said, trying to blink back the pain in his head. "Not the one about how a thousand years ago the people of your village were so poor and hungry that they had to drown their children in the ocean, so the Master of Sinanju had to hire himself out as an assassin to support the village."

Chiun glared. "Not drowned. They were forced to send their babies back to the sea. That is how it is stated: 'Sent back to the sea.' And that was not the legend I was about to relate to you, hoping ever optimistically that I would not be casting my pearls before pale pieces of pigs' ears."

"Okay, okay, already. What's the legend, and what does it have to do with the fact that I slept for seven hours when I never sleep longer than ten minutes?"

"I do not share the legends of my village with Philistines," Chiun said.

Remo sighed. "I'm sorry, Little Father, but this'll have to wait till later. I don't feel right." His own voice sounded far away to Remo, as if he were talking in a cave. He reeled to a far corner of the

13

motel room where they were staying. The air from the room's one window smelled sour.

"Sit down, Remo. You are not yet well."

"I'll be fine. Just need to move around." He curled himself into a loose ball in the corner and began to breathe deeply, expanding out of himself until he lifted himself effortlessly, supported by one hand as his body remained coiled above. Then slowly he unwound first his legs, reaching high into the air with his toes, then his torso. Stretched to full length, Remo bounced once experimentally and then went into the one-and-a-half spin.

He landed clumsily, pulling a muscle in his thigh. Irritated with himself, he got to his feet, but as soon as he was upright, he felt a strange, dark sensation behind his eyes. Then the heavy, drunken sleep that had put him out for so long came back for him again. His legs shivered and buckled. "I can't stop it, Chiun," he said helplessly.

In a moment Remo felt himself being picked up off his feet and carried to the bed. Chiun lay him gently on the covers and wiped Remo's face with clean cloths. "Do not try," the old man's voice called, sounding a thousand miles away. "But you must return, Remo. Understand this. You must return."

As the old voice grew faint and disappeared, Remo found himself back in the sky, again falling through the heavens. His flesh burned. The flames were the only source of light in the vast blackness of space around him. And as he fell, he realized that the light that burned from his charring body was the light of Sinanju, the sun source of all his strength and will. And painful as it was, the light of Sinanju burning in his body was what kept him alive.

14

He had not always been alive, not in the way of Sinanju. A decade before, he had been a Newark cop sentenced to die in the electric chair for a crime he did not commit. After the electrocution, Remo Williams's fingerprints were moved to the dead file, and he had ceased to exist to everyone who cared, which was no one. An orphan with no friends, no family, and no future had died and been reborn in the basement of Folcroft Sanitarium in Rye, New York, under the direction of one Dr. Harold W. Smith.

Dr. Smith needed a man who didn't exist to serve as the enforcement arm of an organization that did not exist, since the function of CURE was to violate the constitution.

CURE was not conceived by thugs or corporate lawbreakers or crime syndicates: these could operate profitably within the Constitution, so they had no reason to violate it. The only group hurt by the Constitution, which had been written long ago as a set of guidelines for decent people to follow, were the decent people themselves, who had become victims of ever-widening crime in America. And so the ultra-secret agency CURE, headed by Dr. Smith, had been developed by a president of the United States just before his death by violent crime.

When Remo awoke that day in Folcroft, he was informed that he no longer existed and taken to meet Chiun, who was to train him in the purest and most ancient method of assassination known to mankind, Sinanju. That day was the beginning of his life, the only life that would matter to him in years to come. For no one, not Dr. Smith, not Chiun, not even Remo himself, had expected the man who did not exist to become anything more

15

than a highly trained killer. They did not know that he would come to absorb Sinanju, to understand and be one with its difficult teachings, that he *was* Sinanju, and that he would become the next Master after Chiun.

On that day, a lifetime ago, Remo Williams assumed his true incarnation, foretold by the most ancient legends of Sinanju. He became Shiva, the god of destruction. Shiva, the Destroyer. Shiva, the dead white night tiger made whole by the Master of Sinanju.

The voice of universes rang out once more. "The legend comes to fruition. In the year of the dragon, a monumental force from the West will seek to destroy Shiva." It rang through the airless depths of space.

And then Remo heard another voice, aged and high, from within himself. That voice said, "You must return."

"I will return, Father," Remo said, and at that moment the sky was filled with light as the monster reappeared, its deadly eyes glowing. It came nearer at blinding speed. Remo watched it come as he fell, unmindful of his burns.

I am Shiva. I burn with my own light. There was no pain. Only readiness.

The dragon attacked, and Remo flowed into the attack, unresisting, adjusting himself to the movements of the beast until he was part of it. Then, with the most gentle of countermovements, he was in the animal's ear, where sound roared through its chambers and off its small bones. Small for a beast the size of an aircraft carrier. The smallest of the bones was as big around as a telephone pole; the largest, the size of a mature Sequoia. Still, he could work here. The confines of the dragon's ear at least provided surface area. Shinnying up the smallest of the ear bones, he felt the animal twitch. Then, as he descended, bringing his feet down at an angle that met with the least resistance, he broke the bone in four places. He did the same to the second and third bones.

By that time, the dragon was stumbling and careening, unable to balance in its flight. It began its drop in space, faster, end over end, and Remo knew the beast was at last dying.

"I can come back now," Remo said. And with an effort of will, he brought himself out of the blackness of space and into a gray mist, where his body felt cold. He shivered.

"Come back," Chiun's voice said. And Remo willed his body to overcome the cold and lie still.

"Awake," Chiun commanded.

Remo opened his eyes slowly. Above him, Chiun hovered, wiping Remo's sweat-drenched brow with silk cloths. "It is done," Chiun said. "You have made the passage safely." Remo tried to rise. "No. Lie still. I will tell you what has happened."

And Chiun told him of the rite of passage all Masters must endure before embarking on the final and most arduous part of their apprenticeship.

"How long will that part last?" Remo asked.

"Twenty or thirty years, for a good pupil. For you, perhaps half a century."

"Swell. Just around the corner. Guess I'd better order my ceremonial robes."

"It is written," Chiun said, ignoring him, "that a force from the West will come to challenge Shiva in the year of the dragon. According to the Korean calendar, that is this year."

17

"Hey. That's what the voice said in my dream."

"I know."

"How do you know what my dream said?"

"Because the voice was mine. The Dream of Death comes to all persons, regardless of their ineptitude, who have mastered the most elementary levels of Sinanju. I saw that you were faltering, so I whispered the legend to give you direction and show you the way home. Had you listened when I attempted to tell you the legend earlier, you would not have had this difficulty."

The phone rang. It was Western Union informing Remo that his aunt Mildred would be arriving at 11 A.M. on Sunday. That meant that Remo was to call Smith at exactly 11 P.M. through the seven-digit code routed through Lexington, Kentucky, Bismarck, North Dakota, and Harrisburg, Pennsylvania before reaching the phone on the desk at Folcroft Sanitarium.

"For Pete's sake," Remo said, hanging up the phone.

"For the emperor's sake," Chiun corrected. "You should not refer to the mad emperor who pays tribute to the Master of Sinanju as 'Pete.' "

"It's just an expression, meaning Smitty's gone on a code rampage again. Aunt Mildred. Nuts."

"It is only logical that the crazed emperor's family would also be crazed. These things are hereditary."

Remo picked up the phone, then put it down again. "Chiun, are we allotted only one dream a lifetime?"

"Would you care to repeat the experience?"

"No."

"Then one dream is enough."

"What was yours about? The dream you had when you were fifteen?"

Chiun looked up at him, his wispy eyebrows arched. "That is a highly personal matter," he said.

"It is? There was nothing personal in my dream."

"Your dream did not bring you shame, thanks to my keen direction."

"You? Shamed? That's a laugh."

"Highly shamed." Chiun's features took on a look of profound suffering. "In my dream I was informed that in the golden years of my life I would be forced to train a white meat eater to take my place as Master."

"That doesn't sound like any Dream of Death to me."

"That is because you are incapable of dying of shame."

Remo dialed the Folcroft number direct. The ring was answered with a surprised "Hello?"

"What's up?" Remo said.

He could hear Smith sputtering at the other end of the line. "It's ten-thirty-one," the bitter, lemony voice snapped. "And what about Aunt Mildred?"

"She told me to give you a message that she left town to become a rock music groupie."

"Very funny. Since you can't keep a secure line, you'll have to meet me at code point a-three-oh-one-five-two." Smith pronounced the code number slowly and precisely. "Repeat, a-three-oh-one-five-two."

"Get off it, Smitty. You know I don't follow your paranoid codes. Tell me in English."

Smith worded his answer carefully. "Where you were sent once before, en route to an encounter two states west with a bald-headed man."

19

Remo scoured his brain. Then it came to him. "Texas?" Remo groused. "Come on. We're in Portland, Oregon. Can't you make it someplace closer?"

Smith exhaled a little gust of air into the telephone. "Make that a-four-one-six-oh-eight," he said quickly. "Look it up in the code book." He hung up.

Cursing, Remo tossed open the telephone directory in the motel room. It was a complex code. The beginning letter indicated the letter of the alphabet under which the location's name would begin. The five numbers following had to be matched to five numbers in the directory. Since Smith had every telephone directory in the country on file in his computer banks in Folcroft, the code could change every time Remo changed location, with little chance it would be detected. Remo's finger slid down the interminable column of numbers under the "A" listing. When he reached 416-0852, he stopped. The first digits matched Smith's code. He moved his finger to the left, to the name "Addison, Charles H." The location was Addison airport. Remo threw the directory on the floor with a crash.

"Where are we going?" Chiun asked.

"Texas," Remo said.

At two A.M. in February, Addison Airport in Galway, Texas, was the bleakest spot Remo could imagine. When the twin-engine Cessna 310 deposited its lone passenger on the otherwise deserted runway, Remo knew why Smith had chosen this as their meeting place. It was because this was the one spot on earth where Smitty looked completely at home.

The lemon-faced man in the gray overcoat, gray wool scarf, gray ten-year-old fedora, and black galoshes walked briskly past Remo and Chiun, to a battered pickup truck. He entered and drove away.

Remo rolled his eyes. "Smitty makes the KGB look like gossips," he said.

"Emperors are always addicted to secrecy."

"Who's going to see us here?" Around them, the freezing Texas wind roared through the deserted airfield. Far, far in the distance, a dim light glowed from the watchman's gate.

They walked over to a late-model pink Cadillac that was sitting where its owner had left it. With a fast three-finger drill on the locking mechanism, Remo jammed it open and got in. Outside, Chiun waited, whistling an old Korean folk tune, his orange robe fluttering in the wind. Remo got out and opened the passenger door. "Excuse me, Little Father, but I thought you would open the door yourself."

"The Master of Sinanju is not a doorman," Chiun said, getting in the car.

Remo went back around to the driver's side and got in. Deftly, he manipulated the wiring, and the car hummed to a start and sped silently out of the airport.

"Right or left?" Remo asked as they approached the road. "Which way'd he go?"

"Right, idiot."

"How do you know?"

"All white men, when given a choice between right and left, veer right. It is an advantage we of the East have had for centuries."

"*We* of the East? You including me?"

"Contain your false if eager pridefulness, o brainless one. 'We' could have referred to any of two billion Oriental persons."

21

"It could have, but it didn't. Admit it, Chiun. You slipped."

The compliment put Remo in a good mood. He hummed as he gunned the Cadillac down the winding Texas road. The name of the tune he was humming was "Disco Lady." He could not recall where he had picked it up, but he remembered some of the words, and sang them:

> Disco Lady
> Won't you be my baby?
> Girl , you got me crazy
> Disco La—

"Halt!" Chiun thundered.

Remo skidded the car to a stop, causing it to swirl in an elaborate loop and careen off the road into a ditch of frozen mud.

"What is it?" Remo whispered, his eyes straining to pierce the darkness miles away.

"It is that revolting melody, with its equally repugnant message."

"Damn it, I drove off the road!" Remo yelled. He got out to look at the damage. "We'll have to lift it out," he said. "It's too deep to push."

"We?" Chiun asked, his hands on his hips.

As Remo was hoisting the two-ton Cadillac back onto the road, the battered pickup truck with Smith at the wheel reappeared, coming from the other direction. The passenger door opened. "Get in," Smith said, his face looking more lemony than usual.

Smith drove silently to a small cabin off the main road and unlocked the door. When Remo and Chiun entered, he was taking off his galoshes. He lit a candle, then removed his hat, coat, and wool scarf. Beneath them he was wearing the three-piece gray suit he had worn every day since Remo had first met him. Sitting at the candlelit kitchen table in the cabin, Smith looked exactly as if he were at his desk in Folcroft Sanitarium.

"A number of men are disappearing from military bases in different parts of the country," he said.

Remo hopped up and sat on the unused wood-burning stove. "C'mon," he said. "They've been doing that since Vietnam. It's called desertion. Or it used to be. Now with this brand-new wacko volunteer army, it's probably one of the new career specialties. Join the army and run away."

Chiun slapped his arm. It stung.

"Silence. Do not speak to our emperor thus," he hissed. "Oh, mighty Emperor Smith, do not punish the young fool too harshly, for he is yet, despite all my effort, a brainless thing. A simple thrashing with wet whips would suffice." He whispered in Korean to Remo, "You deserve to be beheaded, idiot. Let the lunatic emperor talk."

"Nobody gets beheaded in America," Remo said. "It's a good thought, though. Maybe that'd stop the army desertions. We could make a deal with Sweden and Canada. Give them a few bucks for every deserter's head they send back." He shook his head. "They probably wouldn't do it, though. Too bad. The French'd do it. The French'd do anything for a buck. Except work."

"We have reason to believe they're not deserting," Smith said. "In the first place, the missing soldiers aren't recruits. They're chaplains. And nobody knows how they're disappearing or why. According to the president's reports from the Pentagon, none of them took anything with them—no money, no snapshots from home, nothing to indicate that they left voluntarily."

From his vest pocket he extracted a neatly folded map of army bases around the country. Some of the bases were circled, with arrows leading from one to the next. "Fort Antwerth in central Iowa was the first camp to be affected. Then Fort Beson in southern Kansas, followed by Fort Tannehill in New Mexico." He traced the route of the disappearances with his finger. "Whatever's happening, it's moving southward. The next attack, if there is one, should either be at Fort Wheeler in Oklahoma or Fort Borgoyne here in Texas, about a hundred miles due south. You're midway between the two points now. The plane that brought me in has orders to wait for you. You can get to either base in less than an hour."

Remo studied the map. "It could be a nut job," he said.

Smith looked at him drily, awaiting further explanation.

"Some psycho murderer on the outside who doesn't like army preachers," Remo said. "A sniper or something. Can't the army's M.P.'s look into it?"

Smith shook his head. "The reports at all three of the camps where the chaplains disappeared have been negative. Not a trace."

He was silent for a moment, as if deliberating whether or not to tell Remo the rest. After a moment he said, "There's more." He took a miniature tape recorder from his coat pocket.

"Strange things have begun to happen at these camps immediately following the disappearance of their chaplains," Smith said. "The commanders' reports are virtually identical. First, the chaplains disappear. Then there's mass confusion among the enlisted men. For a day or so, the reports are frantic. The officers can't get the recruits to listen to them. Discipline is at zero. Offenders are placed under military arrest, but apparently just about every enlisted man on the base is an offender, and the guardhouses can't hold them all."

"So what do the C.O.'s do then?"

"Nothing. There's nothing they can do but wait for it to pass. At all three camps, the confusion disappeared totally within two or three days. That's been the pattern."

Smith fidgeted in his chair, uncomfortable with what he was saying. "Here's where the reports become really odd," he said quietly, his eyebrows raised. "If this weren't thoroughly documented from three unrelated bases, I'd have difficulty believing it," he waffled.

"Smitty, you have difficulty believing in gravity," Remo said. "Just tell me, and we'll work out the plausibility studies later."

Smith looked at Remo acidly. He took a deep breath. "To a man, the commanders swear that a sweeping change comes over the recruits after the two-or three-day period of chaos. Discipline shoots to an incredible high. Every order is obeyed without question, even the slightest suggestions.

"At Fort Beson, a drill instructor told one of the recruits to go fly a kite. The private wandered off and came back to the identical spot an hour later with a box kite made of newspaper and plywood. He started flying the thing in the middle of dress parade, and wouldn't stop without a direct order."

"That's doing it the army way," Remo said.

Smith's expression was without a trace of humor. "See if this strikes you as amusing," he said, pressing down the "play" button on the recorder.

As the tape began to wind, a man's voice rang tinnily out of the recorder. The man was obviously frightened out of his wits. His voice quavered as he tried to keep it under control. The man was talking wildly about zombies and a foreign plot to take over the U.S. Army, but the focus of the speech was the murder of the man's top aide, a Lieutenant Andrew Fitzroy King. The man on the tape insisted over and over that his aide had been stabbed to death in front of him while he was submitting a report about the weird goings-on at the base.

Smith shut off the recorder. "That was the base commander at Fort Tannehill," he said. "A two-star general. He sent this recording to the president by special courier. The president gave it to me this morning."

"I suppose Lieutenant King disappeared without a trace, too."

Smith closed his eyes and opened them again slowly. "There is no military record of Lieutenant Andrew Fitzroy King on file at the Pentagon," he said. "According to the army, he not only disappeared, he never existed. Of course, I have a few such Kings on file at Folcroft, but I can't determine which one he is, since no one on the base will acknowledge his existence."

"Where's the general now?"

Smith exhaled slowly. "About a half-hour after he sent this tape, he was discovered in a bathtub full of warm water, with his wrists slashed. The report was filed listing it as suicide."

Remo rewound the tape and played it again, listening to the fear in the general's words as they told the bizarre story. He stared thoughtfully at the machine as the general's speech ended and was replaced by a long hiss. After a moment, the recorder clicked off.

"He could have been mentally unbalanced," Remo offered lamely, haunted by the voice on the tape. He wanted to shake the feeling of desperation the general's words had communicated. "Maybe this Lieutenant King person never did exist, as they said."

"I hope you're right," Smith said. "Because if the general was telling the truth, it means that someone's been tampering with the Pentagon files. Only a handful of the most powerful people in the country have private access to those files." The worry lines in Smith's face deepened. He looked very tired.

"Look, Smitty. How sane could the general have been, with that crazy talk about zombies? This guy's suicide probably has nothing to do with the missing chaplains."

"Unfortunately, that's the one word that appears consistently in each of the reports from the bases," Smith said. "Zombies."

He got to his feet and struggled back into his heavy clothes. "Wait here until you hear from me," he said. "This line is secure."

Smith opened the squeaky kitchen door. "By the way, Remo, I expect you to return that car you took from the airport. Automobile theft is a serious offense." He left. In a few moments, the roar of the pickup truck's engine punctuated the still night.

"I'm surprised he didn't make a citizen's arrest," Remo said.

"He should have," Chiun said, rolling out the thin

tatami mat he used for sleeping. "Anyone who drives as you do should be behind bars."

Remo smiled, but his mind was on something else. As he left the house to retrieve the stolen car from the ditch where he had left it, he thought again of the voice on the tape and of the terror behind it. Instinct told him that the general's death was no suicide. Whatever was going on was serious enough to warrant the murder of three chaplains, a commissioned officer, and a base commander.

And Remo had the feeling that this was just the beginning.

Three

Father Malcolm McConnell sighed as he stepped up to the pulpit and looked over his congregation.

The army manual on "Chaplains, Unreasonable Expectations Of," had warned him that the churchgoing rate at an army post was in direct proportion to the soldiers' proximity to enemy bullets, but it had not prepared him for this, not even in peacetime.

The Fort Wheeler Army Chapel was not large, but the spare, boxy hall looked as big as a warehouse this Sunday morning. There was no one inside except for McConnell and the grizzled old sergeant who sat in the second pew.

Where had he gone wrong?

In the beginning, when McConnell had first been transferred to Fort Wheeler, the little chapel had been at least half filled every Sunday, even on the Sunday following the opening of the topless go-go bar in the neighboring town. But in the past two months, attendance had dropped so radically that McConnell was beginning to worry that he had lost his touch.

He tried to revitalize his sermons by focusing on

the zestier episodes of the Bible—the Apocalypse, the Creation of the World, the Song of Solomon—that had always been a hit with his congregations in the past—but he continued to lose his audience despite the racy patter.

He'd practiced his delivery, booming, stage-whispering, pausing for dramatic emphasis. . . . No luck.

In a last-ditch effort, he'd even—God forgive him—hired a pretty 20-year-old folk singer with legs that would stop traffic to play the Meditation on her guitar.

Nothing. The men on the base just weren't interested.

As he watched his flock dwindle from 150 restless recruits to ten reluctant soldiers who'd promised their parents they would go to church come Hell or high water, he became depressed. And when those ten became five, then three, then one, McConnell slipped from depression into despair.

He began to doubt his calling. He had lost his gift. The Lord had entrusted a great many precious souls to him, and he had allowed those souls to drift away. He looked again to the lone soldier occupying his usual spot in the second row, and McConnell's eyes filled with tears. He felt himself an unworthy shepherd, caring for only one lamb.

Struggling to gain control over his emotions, McConnell cleared his throat. The sound echoed through the bare chapel, causing a bird to flutter out of her nest in the rafters and fly chattering over the altar.

"Welcome to the Lord's House, sergeant," He said as cheerfully as he could.

30

"Another big day at Prayerville, Padre, huh?" the sergeant said.

"Looks that way."

It had been looking that way for three weeks running. McConnell lifted his head, searching for a shred of divine inspiration to carry him through the next hour. He saw the bird land on a lamp, look around, then spatter an offering into the fourth row of seats. The sergeant settled into his pew, his arms folded across his chest, his head already beginning to nod.

"Today," McConnell began, forcing his voice to oratory level through sheer strength of will, "we will discuss the mystery of . . . " His voice quivered. "God's Will . . ."

The soldier snored loudly, weaving in his seat.

"Oh, what's the use," McConnell said, and ripped into quarters the notes he'd made for today's sermon. He rested his head in his hands.

The old sergeant frightened himself awake with a snort, his lips smacking sleepily. "Amen," he said.

McConnell stepped off the pulpit and down the three steps leading to the pews. "Do you want me to go through with this, sergeant?" he asked.

The soldier shrugged. "Don't make no difference to me, Father. I just come here out of habit, anyhow. I been going to church every Sunday for twenty years."

Suddenly McConnell felt ashamed of himself for denying the soldier his church service.

"It's kind of a deal I made with the Big Guy up there when my wife got in a bad car crash. They didn't think she'd live, so I made a deal that if she pulled through, I'd go to church every week of my

31

life." He winked and elbowed McConnell in the ribs. "Even if I was the only guy in the church, hey Padre?" McConnell smiled wanly. "Anyways, it ain't right for you to be preaching all by yourself, Father. Looks like the troops went AWOL on you."

"I'll say." McConnell stroked his chin. "Sergeant—ah—"

"Grimes, Father. Bill Grimes."

"Sergeant Grimes, I know this is a little irregular, but I'd like to ask your opinion about how—that is, why—" He blushed.

"How come there ain't nobody here but me, you mean?"

"Exactly. You see, I've been noticing the diminishing attendance, and I've tried literally everything I could to bring the men back to the Church—"

"Oh, the men are in church all right," Sergeant Grimes said with a smile. "These recruits are the goddamndest bunch of churchgoers I run into in twenty-five years in the military. Sunrise services, evening prayer meeting, Wednesday night testimonials, Sunday night communion, Saturday night spirituals—"

"Saturday night? They go to church on Saturday night?"

"Every night of the week, Father. The bunch of them are always in church. They just ain't going to *your* church."

Father McConnell was taken aback. "But this is the army chapel!"

"Beats the hell out of me, too," Grimes said. "Every goddamned night they get all spruced up to walk five miles out of camp to hear some preacher in a goddamned tent, for Christ sake."

"Sergeant," McConnell cautioned.

"Sorry, Padre. It's just that it's the god—the weirdest thing I ever seen." He shook his head. "Sometimes they don't even stick around for mess hall, just so's they can shine up their shoes and head for Reverend Artemis. You ought to see 'em, marching on over that hill at sunset like a pack of zombies. Spooky."

"What did you say the Reverend's name was? Artemis? Like the Greek goddess?"

"Hell of a name for a man of the cloth, ain't it?" Grimes said disgustedly. "These here yo-yo recruits are always trying to get me to go along to prayer meeting or some damn thing with them, but hell, Father, it ain't normal."

"I'm not sure I follow you. What's not normal?"

"It ain't normal for a thousand twenty-year-old recruits to get so all-fired excited about going to church. No offense to your profession, now, but there's sure as hell more ways to get a laugh than by going to prayer meeting, if you ask me."

McConnell saw that he had a point. Even divinity students didn't go to church every day and twice on Sunday. At least Protestants didn't. "Why do you suppose they're all going?" he asked.

The old soldier rose slowly to his feet. "Well, it could be the recruits. Not all there." He tapped his left temple with his finger. "You know, this volunteer army is pulling in some characters I wouldn't trust to cross the street. Back in '44, you wouldn't catch regular army soldiers slinkin' off to church every goddamned minute like a bunch of—"

"Now, sergeant . . . "

"Zombies, I tell you. You just watch them tonight at sunset, marching over that there hill." He pointed eastward, toward the gates of the army bar-

33

racks. "Zombies. Hundreds of them, marching five miles to listen to Reverend Artemis."

"Must be a hell of a preacher," McConnell said, awestruck. "I beg your pardon. A heck of a preacher."

A thousand recruits? Father McConnell tried to picture a cleric who could draw a crowd like that from the brawling, exuberant young soldiers at the base. Whoever this Reverend Artemis was, he had to have the charisma of Moses.

"Zombies," Grimes repeated, pulling McConnell out of his reverie. "Well, seeing as there's no service, I'd like to get back home. The wife's cooking a pot roast." He winked.

"Of course, Sergeant Grimes," McConnell said. "And I'm sorry about the service."

"Don't make no difference. I'll be back next week. That's my deal. Even just you and me, maybe we can play gin."

"Thank you. Thank you very much for telling me about . . . everything."

"Don't mention it." The old soldier sauntered up the aisle.

"Sergeant?"

"Yes, sir."

"Do you think you could bring along a couple of friends next week?" he asked timidly.

"I'll try, but it won't be easy. Most of these zombies would sooner have their legs shot off than miss Reverend Artemis. And that goes for some of the officers, too. They're all in on it. Goddamndest thing I ever seen."

Father McConnell stood still as the soldier's footfalls receded and disappeared behind the closing door. He felt very lonely in the chapel, his chapel, which was once so full of promise.

His mind wandered back to his first commission, as chaplain to a commando unit in Vietnam. He had been scared then, scared from the beginning. When the attacks came thundering out of nowhere and he watched his men being blown to pieces before his eyes, when he'd had to take an M-16 into his own hands and murder a Cong foot soldier to save one of his own men, he'd regretted enlisting, with all his heart.

After that incident, when he discovered for the first time that he was capable of killing another human being, he had wanted to die. He thought of his friends from the seminary, gathered around rock concerts, protesting the war in the safety of the United States, and he wished himself among them, smiling and talking peace with middle class college students. What was he doing in the middle of the jungle, learning how to murder?

It was then that the shell exploded and Father McConnell watched an 18-year-old boy from Mississippi dissolve into flying fragments next to him like a bursting balloon.

The damage from the attack was vast. Twelve men dead, 15 wounded. Most of the wounds were too serious to treat with the unit's exhausted first aid kits. Two of the 15 died minutes after the attack subsided. And in the groaning, bloody sore of a makeshift hospital where the sickly sweet smell of death hung in the air like smoke, Father McConnell realized that he was the only comfort on earth that his men had, and the thought made him boil with rage and hate. He hated the protestors back home in their warm apartments, talking politics over dinner of duckling. He hated the war with its senseless horror day after unrelenting day. He hated the seminary that taught him about communion and confession and absolution and never told him that one August morning an 18-year-old boy was going to blow up in his face.

Father McConnell cried, and he cradled the head of a soldier who had just lost both legs and would probably never leave that stinking, death-sweating jungle, and the soldier cried, too.

Then he prayed. He prayed through the night as he worked feverishly to patch up the holes and cuts on the bodies of his men. He prayed the next day as he dug the graves where his dead would be buried. He prayed as he crawled with the survivors, dragging the man who now had no legs through the jungle marshes. He prayed loud, so that all his men would hear him; and he prayed often, because that was all they had.

And when the war was over, the man who had no legs miraculously was still alive. He told Father McConnell that the priest had saved his life.

And then Father Malcolm McConnell understood why he had joined the army.

His thoughts returned to the empty chapel. This was going to be where he made his home, serving the soldiers who served their country. But the soldiers didn't need him now, it seemed.

Maybe he just didn't have it anymore. The recruits weren't denying God. They were simply ignoring Father Malcolm McConnell, which was certainly their prerogative, especially since this Reverend Artemis was doing the job of ten Father McConnells.

He tried to fight the feelings of envy that rose in his throat as he left the chapel. He tried to maintain a cheerful dignity in the mess hall as he ate his dinner alone, while the soldiers at the adjoining tables extolled the virtues of Father Artemis. He tried to tell himself that God's will was sometimes difficult to understand, as he sat on the grassy hill at sunset, watching an army of young soldiers march past him toward the gates leading from the base.

They were going to Father Artemis.

With blinding clarity, Father McConnell knew what he must do. He would go to Father Artemis, too.

In one swift motion, McConnell was on his feet and marching with the recruits through the gates. *If you can't beat 'em, join 'em*, he thought. He would find out what made Father Artemis such a sensation with the troops. Oh, the man was undoubtedly more talented a speaker than McConnell was, but just watching Father Artemis in action might help to bring at least a few recruits back to the little army chapel.

"Hey!" a freckle-faced young man called. "It's McConnell!"

"Glad you got the spirit, McConnell," another young recruit said, rumpling the priest's hair like a puppy dog's.

"*Father* McConnell," he corrected.

"Don't worry, McConnell. Artemis is all-loving. Even heretics like you he will take into his heart."

"Reverend Artemis," he corrected again, but no one seemed to hear him.

The services were being held in a huge striped

37

circus tent bearing the words PRAISE ARTEMIS in five-foot-high block letters. The tent was set up in a remote spot in the desert.

The congregation that waited for Father Artemis was packed to bursting inside the hot, airless tent. There were no seats inside, and the stifling desert heat, combined with the sweat of more than a thousand bodies, very nearly caused Father McConnell to pass out. He would have sunk to the floor, had there been room. As it was, he bobbed and weaved upright, supported by the crush of the surrounding congregation.

From across the massive tent someone shouted, "Praise Artemis!" and a thousand voices took up the chant.

"Praise Artemis!" they called, clapping their hands in rhythm. "Praise Artemis!" they screamed, stomping their feet. "Praise Artemis!" they cheered, their bodies convulsing crazily, their eyes rolling in ecstasy.

"This can't be true," Father McConnell whispered as the mob whipped themselves into a frenzy.

The cheering was interrupted by shrieks and applause, which grew and swelled throughout the tent as a man and woman appeared at the side entrance. The crowd parted as the two of them climbed onto a platform set up in the front beneath a "Praise Artemis" sign painted in pink Day-Glo letters.

The man was the strangest looking pastor Father McConnell had ever seen. He sported shoulder-length blond hair, the ends of which curled over the shoulder of a snow-white toga trimmed in rhinestones. In his right hand he carried a sparkling trident. In his left he carried a white neon lightning bolt. He looked like a football player on his way to the Beaux Arts ball.

He raised his implements into the air as a sign that the services were about to begin. The crowd went wild. Smiling broadly, he handed the trident and the lightning bolt to the woman, who was similarly attired in diaphanous white gauze, which silhouetted her curvaceous body in awesome detail. The woman knelt to receive the props, exposing a scandalous portion of her ample bosom.

"Good Lord," Father McConnell said in spite of himself.

Reverend Artemis posed like a statue as the roar of the crowd subsided. The woman blew Dinah Shore kisses to the troops.

"My children," Artemis intoned, "we are gathered here this evening to praise the holy name of the one true God."

"Praise God!" the recruits shouted.

"And to condemn the evildoers who worship falsely."

"Death to the false gods!" the recruits screamed.

"For our nation is plagued with the evil spread by the false gods and their demented followers."

"Death to the followers of the false gods!"

Father McConnell noticed that the recruits were reading their responses from huge cards held by the woman on stage.

"And only through the strength of our military might may we hope to banish evil from our land."

"Praise God!" they shouted. "Hail Artemis!"

Father McConnell could not believe his eyes. That was what it said on the card: "Hail Artemis."

"Hail Artemis!" they yelled. "Hail Artemis!"

"No," McConnell whispered. "Oh, dear God . . ."

He began to back away through the press of bodies toward the exit, but he was restrained by two burly soldiers carrying billy clubs.

"Let me go!" Father McConnell hissed. Instead he felt the cold metal of handcuffs slapping shut over his wrists, and felt his body borne high above the heads of the congregation as the guards carried him forward.

"What have we, o sentries?" Artemis boomed. The crowd was still.

"A heretic, most exalted Lord Artemis, God of Gods." They set McConnell down at the feet of the white-robed pastor.

"What say you?" Artemis boomed, staring at McConnell.

Father McConnell cleared his throat to speak. No sound came out. He tried again. "I am Father Malcolm McConnell of the Roman Catholic faith, chaplain to the Fort Wheeler United States Army Base," he said. His pronouncement was met with boos and Bronx jeers and shouts of "Infidel!"

"Are you come to make amends for your evil existence as a tool of the corporate-military oppressors?" Artemis asked.

"I most certainly am not," McConnell said. "What you are practicing is blasphemy, and it cannot be condoned—"

"Death to the evil messengers of false gods!" someone screamed so loudly that his voice cracked. And then the tent was teeming with enraged soldiers stampeding toward the handcuffed priest.

"Halt!" Artemis said, raising the neon lightning bolt offered by the woman in white. Instantly, silence fell over the throng. "Clear the circle. It is time."

A hushed buzz filled the tent. "Time for what?" Father McConnell asked, feeling his sweat pouring from his armpits. "Time for what?" he repeated.

A lone soldier worked his way through the crowd to the edge of the circle surrounding Father McConnell. It was Sergeant Grimes. His hands were in his pockets, and he smiled. "Exorcism," he said softly. "That's what the Sunday evening services are for. I was in charge of getting you here, devil priest."

Father McConnell's eyes widened. "Sergeant Grimes," he whispered.

"Your kind's not long for this world," he said. "Not if we have anything to do about it." A buzz of assent circulated around the sweltering tent.

Artemis raised his hands for silence, and the crowd was still. "Before we cast out the evil in the demon follower of the false god, we will purify ourselves with the taking of the Cup," he intoned. The woman in white scurried behind a curtain and reappeared with an enormous silver chalice filled with red liquid. Artemis took it by its two handles and spoke in a voice of deepest authority.

"You are the soldiers of Artemis, about to take the first step toward destroying the oppressors of this nation," he said. "The flag of America proves its devil worship by bearing thirteen stripes. From the beginning has it been a repository of evil on earth. You did not enter this army to die for the devil-worshipping politicians."

"No," came the thundering response.

"You did not enter this army to march into distant lands to wage war on innocents."

41

"No," the men yelled, looking as one thousand-eyed animal at the cup in Artemis's hands.

"You did not enter this army to see your nation's poor and helpless beaten by the corporate-political system."

"No!"

"And now I ask you: Why did you enter this army?"

The recruits looked among themselves, bewildered. "I will tell you," Artemis whispered. The crowd listened raptly. "You joined the army to find the one true way."

Cheers.

"Put your faith in me, o Lambs of Artemis, and I will show you the road to glory."

"Praise Artemis," they shouted.

"I will take you all to a promised land, where you may serve men of greatness. Even as I speak, that land is opening up to you, awaiting your triumphant entry. And that land shall be called Vadassar."

The room buzzed with excitement. "Hail Vadassar!" the men shouted.

"Vadassar will be your home and your strength."

"Hail Vadassar."

"Vadassar will be your master and your servant."

"Hail Vadassar."

Father McConnell looked up, puzzled, at Artemis's fiery eyes. What on earth was Vadassar?

"One day, my children, I will be gone from this world, but Vadassar shall remain to carry on my work through eternity. When I die, Vadassar will provide for you." Artemis held the cup before him at arm's length. "Therefore, this do in remembrance of me," he said, his eyes ceilingward. "With this Cup will you find Vadassar and serve it well."

42

"This is madness," Father McConnell said, crossing himself. A soldier slapped his hands down.

The men formed a single line to approach Artemis and his chalice of murky liquid. One by one, they drank from it, and as they did, their eyes took on a vacant stare, their jaws sagged open, and they wandered aimlessly around the tent, not speaking, not focusing, mindlessly walking into one another like bumper cars.

"Behold the devil priest!" Artemis roared, pointing to the trembling Father McConnell at his feet.

The men formed a circle around him. "Out, demon, out," they chanted. Their voices were low. They inched forward menacingly. "Out, demon, out."

"This is the United States of America," McConnell pleaded. "You can't do this."

"Out, demon, out." The circle tightened.

"Come to your senses!"

"Out, demon, out." The white-robed woman with Artemis fell to her knees. "Out, demon, out," she moaned, tearing her gossamer gown to her waist, exposing her fleshy breasts. Her nipples were pink and hard. She writhed on the floor at Artemis's feet, beside McConnell.

"She's picked up his spirit," Artemis yelled. "We have a true demon in our midst, spreading his evil filth to the prophetess Samantha."

Screams of outrage filled the night as the men closed in, zombielike, and the prophetess Samantha stripped, wriggling, to the buff. "Out, demon, out," she called breathlessly as she bucked and thrashed on the floor.

"As we do to you, priest, so shall we do to all who serve the oppressors of men," Artemis shrieked.

Father McConnell closed his eyes and repeated the Pater-Noster for the last time.

With a heave, Artemis lifted the prophetess Samantha out of the way as the recruits fell in a wave on the trembling form of Father Malcolm McConnell. When they were done, the priest was little more than a smear on the dirt floor of the tent.

"And whosoever here shall betray himself or others shall die," Artemis concluded in final warning against anyone present who might still be entertaining the notion of discussing the evening's activities with someone outside the holy order.

"Praise Artemis," the prophetess Samantha chanted weakly as the remains of Father McConnell were being covered with sawdust.

"Praise Artemis!" the troops cheered, tossing paper money at their new god while Samantha, naked as a jaybird, blew them kisses.

"Wow, that was a hot one," Samantha murmured under the roar of the crowd.

"Shit," Artemis said. "I missed out on the action, as usual."

Four

"Oklahoma," the fatigued, lemony voice on the telephone said. "The chaplain from Wheeler was reported missing this morning. It must have happened last night."

Remo and Chiun were stopped at the gate by two sentries who looked as if they were experiencing the final stage of narcotics poisoning. "Where you going, man?" one of them asked, scratching his crotch.

"How about straight ahead?" Remo took out his wallet and rummaged inside for appropriate identification. The Department of Agriculture card would have sufficed, but the guard held out a shaky hand. "Wait, mister. You from the devil-worshipping socio-industrial-corporate oppressors?"

"What?"

"You from the—"

"Never mind," Remo said. "Whatever you said, we're not from there. My friend here's a student nurse. We've come to pick up a few pointers on ptomaine poisoning from the mess hall."

"Enter," the guard said.

Remo looked over his shoulder at the guards as he trotted inside. One was nodding off, his forehead resting against the barrel of his rifle. The other was staring fixedly at the sun. "Say, can either of you tell us the way to the administration building?"

The nodder snapped to with a lazy jerk of his head. "Uh," he said, trying vainly to retract his tongue into his face, "I think it's a white building. Mostess administration buildings be white. Always a white building when I go to get my food stamps or the welfare. Once, when they was gonna make me an administrator in the CETA program, they sent me to an administration building, and that one was white too. And when the judge tell me I gots join the army or gets twenty years, that be in a white building too. Yup, you just find yourself a white building. That be the administration building."

Remo glanced around.

"All the buildings are white," he said.

The guard roused himself enough to look around. A small furrow appeared between his eyes. "Lookie, lookie," he said, astonished. "Every last one of them. Hey, Wardell." He prodded his associate, who continued to gaze, unblinking, at the white Oklahoma sun. "Wardell, lookie here. All these buildings be white. Hey, Wardell." Wardell stared on.

"Thanks a lot," Remo said, as he and Chiun walked away toward the mass of white buildings clustered ahead.

"These are the fighting men Emperor Smith employs to defend your country?" Chiun asked.

"Yeah," Remo said.

"No wonder you lost against even the Vietnamese. The first recorded war victory in the long, lamentable history of those duck-romancers."

46

"Uh huh," Remo said. "Our army didn't lose Vietnam. The rest of the country gave up. Not the army. But that was the old army. This is the new army. These are all volunteers."

"This, then, is their chosen work?" Chiun asked.

" 'Fraid so, Chiun."

"Now I understand."

"Understand what?"

"How Emperor Smith finds you to be even moderately useful. Look at what he has to compare you with."

"That's interesting," Remo said. "I always thought he compared me with you and found me witty, charming, sensible, intelligent, and a perfect delight to have around."

"Heh, heh," Chiun said. "I've always told you that Smith is a lunatic, but I never told you he was a fool. He would not be likely to compare a chip of glass with a diamond and choose the chip of glass. Heh, heh."

Chiun looked around. The expression on his face would have been appropriate for watching babies being boiled. "How long has your army been like this?"

"A few years," Remo said. "We used to have an army like everybody else; when we needed soldiers, we drafted them. To protect their country, people came. Then some genius decided it was too much to expect anybody to sacrifice anything for his country, and they changed the army to all volunteers."

"So these people fight not for love of country, but for a paycheck?" Chiun asked.

"That and to stay out of jail or because they've used up every other kind of government check they could get without working."

"It'll never work," Chiun said.

"It doesn't," Remo said.

"Now the Persian Army," Chiun said.

"Good?"

"So-so. The Master at that time helped them, and so they made short work of their enemies. But volunteers were not allowed. The emperor of the Peacock Throne knew that soldiers should be unwilling recruits. Only then will they be angry enough to fight well. The Carthaginians too. They were better. They had a Master of Sinanju too, and he did most of the fighting while they played their lutes and drums. Thus developed the Carthaginian victory at Bothay." Chiun raised an index finger in the air. "But no Carthaginian ever deserted."

Just then, a young recruit came walking toward them. He stared straight ahead, and his arms hung limply at his sides as he strode in even paces toward the gate.

"Excuse me, soldier," Remo said. But the recruit walked past him without missing a step.

"Rude," Chiun said. "He must be a Cypriot."

"He's an American soldier," Remo said irritably. "And he's stoned, to prove it. Well, anyway, there's someone else up ahead we can ask."

About 20 yards away, two soldiers stood talking. "Hey, fellas," Remo said, but they must not have heard him, because as he approached, one of them drew a Bowie knife from his uniform and plunged it into the heart of the other.

"Wait a second," Remo said, racing ahead to collar the attacker. "What the—" But even as he spoke, the soldier with the knife stabbed himself in the chest, hara-kiri style. He slumped to the ground, a thin smile playing on his lips.

"Hey. You." Remo shook the still-warm corpse, whose eyes were already glazing over.

"Your American army behaves abominably," Chiun said. "The angle of his elbow was completely incorrect. It was merely luck that he managed to accomplish his task, even at such close range and with such an unnecessary weapon." He shook his head. "Tsk. Disgraceful."

Just then a lean, athletic-looking major with a team of six soldiers in full combat dress surrounded the two bodies. The major looked briefly at Remo and Chiun, then directed his men toward the entrance gates. Remo noticed that the soldiers all looked straight ahead as they marched in perfect rhythm.

"Everybody looks mindless around here," Remo observed.

"Of course," Chiun said with a small smile of triumph.

"Why 'of course'?"

"They are white. Mindlessness is natural to those of your race."

"Two of those soldiers were black."

"Black skin, tan skin, pink skin," Chiun said with a dismissive wave. "All non-yellow persons behave as one in America."

Remo ignored him. "I guess that's the administration building over there. I see typewriters in the windows."

A guard stood in front of the big white building. His eyes, too, were vacant. Remo waved a hand in front of the guard's face, but his stare was unblinking. They walked past him and climbed automatically to the top floor of the building, where the bellowing bass voice of someone behind a door labeled

49

"General Arlington Montgomery" drowned out all the other noise on the floor.

"I'm damned if I know what's going on, Major. It's your job to tell me everything I know. Now you find out where that pansy chaplain went to, or you stay on latrine duty till the day you retire." A telephone jingled as it slammed into its cradle.

Inside, a middle-aged WAC sat typing. She looked up coldly.

"Hi. We're here to see the general," Remo said.

"Do you have an appointment?" Without waiting for an answer, she began to type again.

"I don't think we need one," Remo said as he slid two fingers to the base of her ear. The WAC nuzzled and purred like a kitten. "More," she said. "Are you an officer?"

"No. I was in the army once, but I was a private."

She leaped out of her chair with a clatter and assumed a karate stance. "A *private*?" She brushed imaginary germs off her neck. "Ugh. Touched by a private. Get out of here before I have you exterminated."

"Ah, gentle lady," Chiun said, smiling sweetly, "I can see you are a person of rare discernment, meant only for the finer offerings of this life."

"Oh, really?" she said, cocking her head coquettishly. "How can you tell?"

"It is written on your lovely visage, reminiscent of the flowering jasmine which blooms on the shores of my native village." As Chiun settled into a chair beside the WAC, who was now looking at herself in a compact mirror, Remo walked through the door to the general's office.

"Howdy," he said.

"How the hell did you get in here?"

50

"Your guards are out to lunch, and your secretary's establishing relations with North Korea."

"What? Why aren't you in uniform? Where are you from?"

"Listen, let's cut the formalities. I'm here to find out about the missing chaplain."

A look of shock passed over the general's face. "How do you know about that? Who sent you?"

"The Pentagon. All very hush-hush. They want me to talk to only the best-informed and most intelligent of their field generals. Just between you and me, Arlington, there could be a big promotion in this for whoever turns over the hottest leads on this problem."

"Europe? You mean Europe?"

Remo winked. "Could be."

The general cleared his throat. "Well, let's see. It's my opinion that we must first explore the parameters of this situation and determine the possible consequences of our actions in this matter before undertaking—"

"You don't know doodly squat, do you?"

The general bristled. "I have a theory," he said defensively.

"What's that?"

The general leaned close to Remo and lowered his voice conspiratorially. "They're unionizing."

"Who?"

"The foot slogs. Discipline is at an all-time low. They don't march in formation. They don't wake up on time. When you try to get them to do anything, they just stare off into space."

"Why don't you throw them in the slammer?"

"The guardhouse is full. The stockade's full. There's no place else to put them. And the craziest

51

thing is, they don't mind being locked up. When they're arrested, they just trot off happy as pie. This new army's just a mess of worthless jelly bellies. They couldn't fight if their lives depended on it."

"I don't know about that. I just saw one of your privates murdering another one. Right outside your window, in fact."

"Is that your idea of a joke, boy?" The general's face grew red. His jowls shook. "Now, I've been hearing all those reports about the other bases, but I mean to tell you, Senate spy or whoever you are, that I run a tight ship here. There's been no hanky panky since that chaplain wandered off last night. And I won't have you going back to Washington with horror stories about Fort Wheeler and General Arlington Montgomery."

"Suit yourself. You'll get a report on it soon enough. One guy killed the other with a knife, and then he killed himself. There were seven witnesses."

In a fury, the general punched one of the buttons on his speakerphone. "You're going to eat your words, boy," he sputtered. "Get Major Van Dyne in here. On the double."

"Yes, sir," the WAC said between giggles.

"This had better be on the level, mister, or you're in big trouble. With those candy-ass liberals in Washington, and with me."

"Saw it with my own eyes," Remo said, smiling.

Major Van Dyne appeared in the doorway, carrying a walkie-talkie. His uniform was crisp and knife-pleated. He was the same officer who'd had the bodies removed from the grounds. "Yes, sir," he said, saluting.

"Do you know anything about a stabbing incident on the entrance grounds?"

"And a suicide," Remo added helpfully.

"No, sir."

"Hey, wait a second," Remo said, approaching the major. "You were there. You witnessed it. The crazy guy with the Bowie knife, who sliced up his buddy and then sent himself to happy land, remember?"

"I've never seen this man before in my life, sir," the major said. Remo noticed that his eyes held the same faraway look the guards' had. "I suggest we place this person under arrest."

The major spoke into his walkie-talkie. "Two unidentified civilians in General Montgomery's office."

"Just as I thought," the general said. "Another crackpot sent by those left-wing apostles of surrender in Washington. Well, let me tell you, wise guy, I'm going to teach you and those faggots at the Pentagon that it doesn't pay to mess with Old-Blood-and-Guts."

"Want to go down in American military history?" Remo asked.

"How's that?" Montgomery asked.

"Call yourself Old-Guts-and-Blood. You'll be the first. Everybody and his brother calls himself Old-Blood-and-Guts."

"Lock him up."

"I thought you didn't have room in the guardhouse," Remo said.

"For you, we'll make room. Now get out of here."

At a signal from Major Van Dyne, the six combat soldiers rushed in, grabbing Remo around his neck and chest. He slipped away easily. "No, no," he said. "No touchie, no feelie, guys." They lunged

53

at him again. One of the men upended his rifle to smash the butt into Remo's face. It missed and crashed into the wall behind.

As the soldier was pulling the barrel out of the wall, Remo took it between two fingers like a baton, dispatching the soldier at the other end and a corporal standing nearby, who had a bayonet aimed at Remo's belly. With a flick of his toe, he turned a third combat soldier's spine to jelly. The fourth drew a small hand pistol and fired it at Remo, but since Remo had placed himself in a direct line with a soldier who was coming at him from behind with a knife, he weaved out of the way the instant he saw the soldier's trigger finger move, and there was no longer anyone behind him, at least no one with a face. The last soldier fired twice more before his hand was missing. Then his arm was missing. Then, after a quick tap to his forehead, his life was missing.

"Now, suppose you and I talk, Major," Remo said. With unseeing eyes, Major Van Dyne stared straight ahead at Remo as he pulled out the walkie-talkie he carried. "Intercept and detain," he said into it. In a swift motion, Remo was behind him, pressing the nerves along the base of his spine, and the walkie-talkie clattered to the floor.

"Talk," he said. But all he could get out of the major was something that sounded like "Hail Artemis."

"Crackpots," the general said. "Crackpots to the right of me. Crackpots to the left of me. What the hell's he saying?"

"Beats me," Remo said, and sent the major to paradise with a crack of his upper vertebrae.

The general surveyed the mass of twisted, bloodied bodies in his office. "Best damn fighter I've seen since Guadalcanal," he said. "Where'd you learn hand to hand combat, Vietnam?"

"Close enough."

"You a Russky?"

"I'm an American," Remo said.

"Damn glad to hear it, son. An American who can fight. Warms the heart."

"Aren't you afraid I'm going to kill you?"

"Hell, I expect you will. I called for more troops while the ruckus was going on, but you're faster than they are. Hell, I can't even get the bastards out of bed anymore."

Far in the distance, Remo could hear the sound of marching feet approaching the building. It had to be the general's replacement troops, Remo reasoned.

"All right, get on with it," the general said, assuming a fighting stance, his portly belly jiggling in front of him. "To tell the truth, I feel pretty silly doing this after all these years, but it's a better way to go than having some idiot recruit misfire his weapon into me during target practice. Get on with it." He formed his features into a combat scowl. "Arghh. Arghh."

"What's that?"

"Mad noises. Scares hell out of the enemy. Arghh."

"Calm down, General," Remo said, writing down some numbers on a piece of paper. "Here's where you can reach me in case you find out anything. Van Dyne was in on whatever's going on around here, and I don't think he was alone. Do the country a favor and tell me about any leads you get before you tell any more of your majors."

55

The general followed Remo to the anteroom, where the WAC was batting her eyelashes and attempting to show Chiun a portion of her thigh. "Let's go," Remo said, and in less than a second the general saw the thin young man who could fight so well and an unknown aged Oriental go out the window and shinny down the sheer face of the building.

"Let me know if you want to enlist," the general called out the window after them. "You can start as a corporal."

Five

Toward the end of his descent down the building, Remo's leg brushed against the chest of a tall, leggy redhead. Her two-piece khaki uniform looked like evidence that the modern army had decided to open up a supply room on Rodeo Drive in Beverly Hills.

"Quite a trick," she said. She looked appraisingly at the smooth wall.

"Something I picked up at summer camp," Remo said.

"You've got a lot of nerve, you know."

"Naah, not really. If you can climb up it, you can climb down it. It's not hard."

"Do not reveal the secrets of Sinanju to outsiders," Chiun cautioned in Korean.

"I didn't mean the wall," the girl said. "I mean you have a lot of nerve copping a free feel like that."

Remo looked around at the expanse of ground surrounding them. "If God didn't want your chest rubbed, he wouldn't have given you enough for two. Anyway, you could have stepped out of the way."

"Then I wouldn't have enjoyed it as much." Her

57

face broke into a pretty smile. Her eyes were jade green. "Work here?"

"Sort of. See you."

Remo and Chiun turned the corner. The girl ran ahead of them. They brushed past her without slowing. "Hey," she called. "I won't bite. My job is to make visitors feel at home here. Public relations." The breeze blew the scent of her perfume into Remo's nostrils. It smelled woodsy and sensual.

"We do not relate to the public," Chiun said.

"That's a beautiful robe," the redhead said, tentatively touching Chiun's kimono. "You can always tell hand-brocaded silk."

Chiun stopped and said, "Remo, don't keep walking while this lady is talking to us." To the woman, he explained, "Rude. He has no manners. Ignore him. The women of my village toiled long to make this robe. It is perfect."

"I can see that. It suits you well."

"The Master of Sinanju always cloaks himself in perfection," Chiun said with a smile.

"What was that about giving away secrets?" Remo asked.

Chiun sniffed at him. "Unfortunately, so few things on the earth are perfect. It can be disheartening for one who seeks after beauty and truth to be surrounded with loutishness and ingratitude."

"How very sad. But the grinding that would wear a lesser stone to nothing only serves to give luster to a diamond."

Chiun beamed. "True. Very true. You are a wise child. She is very wise, Remo. Proof that some whites can think."

"Come on, Little Father," Remo said. "She's playing you like a harp."

The girl continued, "I didn't make it up. My father always says that."

"Your father is Korean?" Chiun asked.

"I'm afraid not, but he does what he can."

Chiun nodded sympathetically. "He might be nice anyway."

"Well, it's been swell," Remo said, taking Chiun by the elbow. The Oriental yanked his arm away.

"Unhand me, lout," he said. "Do you see how I must suffer at the hands of my ungrateful pupil who does not even recognize a pure spirit when he encounters one? Tell me again, child, about the grinding."

She smiled at Remo. "The grinding that would wear a lesser stone to nothing—"

"My grinding teeth are wearing away to nothing," Remo said. "Could we at least move away from here? The place'll be crawling with zombies in a minute."

"That's a great idea," the redhead said. "How about my place?"

"Alas, I must return to our dwelling," Chiun said, "for I am weary from lack of sleep. Perhaps we shall meet again to discuss other adages of your respected father's." He tottered away, wiping his brow weakly.

"He's precious," the girl said to Remo. "You ought to take better care of that frail old man."

Out of the corner of his eye, Remo saw Chiun walking in a collision course with another of Fort Wheeler's automaton soldiers. When the soldier neglected to give way before the Master of Sinanju, he was flattened into the dirt by Chiun's flailing right hand.

"I'll remember to be more gentle with him," Remo said.

"Now how about my place?"

"Thanks, but I've got some work to do."

"Maybe I can help. Try me."

Remo shrugged. "Know anything about a missing chaplain?"

"He was murdered, most likely. Just like the chaplains at Antwerth, Beson, and Tannehill."

"Not bad. What else do you know?"

"I'll tell you in bed, Brown Eyes."

The redhead in the captain's uniform lived off the base in a sprawling ranch house furnished in brass and satin.

"Nice place," Remo said. "I guess army salaries are higher than they used to be."

The girl laughed. "This isn't army issue. Daddy rents my living quarters for me while I'm on the road."

"Then I take it you've been to the other bases where people have been disappearing."

"That's right."

"And you're not in public relations, are you?"

"Army intelligence. I'm here to investigate the same things you are."

"And who's Daddy?"

"Osgood Nooner. Senator Osgood Nooner, the champion of human rights. You've seen him on TV. Your three questions are up."

She unbuttoned her jacket and blouse in front of Remo and stepped out of her skirt easily. Her flesh was creamy, and her red hair fell to her nipples. "I'm Randy," she said throatily as she put her hands on him.

"I can tell."

60

"That's my name, silly. Randy Nooner. What about you?"

"Call me Remo," he said, as she led him to a plush bedroom dimly lit by soft pink light.

"I'm glad we know each other, Remo. I never have sex with strangers."

"It's good to know there are still some women who hold out for a meaningful relationship."

Randy wiggled and pinched and probed and caressed and otherwise irritated Remo, who just wanted her to hold still so he could get the whole boring process over with. Along with not being able to sleep, dream, or sweat, Remo had acquired a problem with women as a result of his training with Chiun. For someone who at one time had drooled at the sight of a pretty tush, Remo's interest in fooling around with girls had dwindled to near nonexistence. Sinanju had done that.

Early in his training, Remo had learned the fifty-two steps toward bringing a woman to ecstasy, although he'd never encountered a woman who could hang on past step 11 before coming in a frenzy. His concentrated technique assured him that the women he was with would end up satisfied, but since the same technique left Remo yawning, sex just didn't have the same kick as it used to.

"You're really a beautiful person, Remo," Randy said, squeezing off all circulation to his privates.

"Yeah," Remo said as he touched her in a place beneath her left armpit that sent her into shrieks of pleasure. He was thinking that he hadn't eaten since noon the day before. "Say, is there a grocery store around here?"

He manipulated her calf muscles with a flutter of

his fingers. "Oooh," she moaned. "What do you want to eat, baby? Huh? Huh?"

Remo's eyes wandered ceilingward. This one wasn't going to get past step 4. Well, at least it would be out of the way quickly.

"Huh?" she persisted, clawing at his chest. "Tell me what you want in your mouth. I'll give it to you. I'll give it to you good, honey. Oooh."

"Well, actually, I was thinking about rice. And maybe a little duck." He worked his fingers up to her thigh.

"Oh, duck!" Her head flailed wildly, whipping cascades of red hair into Remo's mouth. "Duck, oh, duck, baby," she yelled, frothing and shaking like a mad thing.

As she lay panting and sated, Remo listened to the little gurgle of hunger in his stomach. He silently cursed Chiun for developing him into a man whose major preoccupation in a woman's bed was a bowl of rice.

"You've certainly got some funny bedroom patter, Remo."

"Sorry."

"Don't apologize, darling. It drove me wild. I felt like you were so—so real."

"Uh huh. Suppose we could talk about the missing chaplains?"

"I'd rather talk about us."

"Okay. What do we know about the missing chaplains?"

She sighed. "Men. You're all alike. Just worried about getting your rocks off. If there's one thing I can't stand, it's sexual selfishness."

"Okay, then, forget it," he said, throwing his legs over the bed. "It's been swell."

"You mean you're not coming back?"

"We don't seem to communicate."

"They're being killed off by the recruits. Now get back in here."

"Why?"

"Because they're the wrong religion. Do it to me again, Remo lover. Lay that duck stuff on me."

"What's the right religion?"

"According to the men, some traveling evangelist a few miles out of town. I was going to check it out tonight. Services are at eight. Go to it, Remo. Down this way." She led his hand to her inner thigh, where he had left off.

"What about the others who've been getting killed? I saw somebody murdered today."

"I guess they're the wrong religion, too," she said. "Look, if I had this thing all sewn up, I wouldn't be down here investigating. That's all I know, so sock it to me."

"Later," Remo said, gliding into his trousers. "I've got to get to some duck before church tonight."

Randy sat up abruptly, teeth bared. "Why, of all the cheap, no good, low down, male chauvinist . . . Ooooh."

Remo had slid his hand to a spot just to the right of her spinal column and pressed two nerves together until they locked in exquisite pleasure. "There," he said. "That'll hold you for an hour or so, until the nerves relax. Then you'll fall into a gente sleep. So long."

"Duck," she rumbled, beating the mattress with her fists. "Duck, Remo. Oh, duck."

* * *

Remo finished his duck and changed into the black T-shirt and tan chinos he had bought at the airport. They were identical to the clothes he'd worn the day before, but working assassins weren't paid to hang around laundromats, so he bought new clothes whenever he had the time to change.

That was the deal Smith had made him more than a decade before—all expenses for the remainder of his working life, and all the spending money he wanted. What Smith didn't tell him was that men who don't exist don't need a lot of money. Flashy clothes and jewelry would only be an encumbrance; buying a car would be a waste of time, since he'd had to abandon every car he'd driven since he began working for Smith; and he would never be able to own a permanent home or raise a family. Chiun was the only family he had ever known, or would ever know.

He looked at himself in the mirror on the wall of the motel room where he was staying. He realized, with a little surprise, that he possessed the kind of face women would find attractive. The high cheekbones, the deep-set brown eyes, the firm mouth—it was a better face than the one he had been born with. Less vulnerable looking, perhaps. The Brazilian plastic surgeons Smith had hired the first time Remo's identity had been compromised had been skillful and experienced, with an eye for masculine beauty.

The lean body was unrecognizable from the one Remo had when he was a young policeman, before his training with Chiun began. That body had been fleshy and muscular. This one was deceptively thin. Only the unusually thick wrists—a genetic "flaw" that had become a great asset in climbing and fighting—remained.

Still, he wondered, who was Remo Williams? Gone, as forgotten as an obscure line from an obscure play. Would he have been happy living as a normal man with normal weaknesses, with friends to swap lies with and a woman to love? He would never know.

He turned away. Mirrors always brought out the fool in him. Who needed mirrors, anyway?

The phone rang. "Yeah," he said. The wire was silent but for strained breathing at the other end. "Who is this?"

"Vadassar," came the strangled response.

"Who?"

"Montgomery," the voice managed.

"General? Is that you? What is it?"

"Vadassar. The recruits. Zombies . . ." The general's voice was weakening. "They're—" He gasped, choking for air. "They're going to kill us all," he said. Then Remo heard the receiver drop to a hard surface, and there was no more sound.

What he found at Fort Wheeler resembled the Vietnamese villages he'd seen during the war. Bodies were everywhere, their bellies slit open, their heads blown away, littering the base grounds like broken toys. The only sound Remo could hear was the eerie, faraway howling of coyotes. As he stepped over the corpses, Remo noticed that almost all of them wore the uniforms of top officers.

The administration building was worse. The mutilated remains of human beings who evidently had been going about their daily work were strewn over

65

the stairwells and on the floors, now slippery with blood. Clipboards and brown-spattered sheets of paper lay scattered beside them. An open elevator exposed the fragments of its last passengers, who had been grenaded out of existence until they were no more than bits of flesh and cloth dotting the walls. Through each open office door he saw the dead, grotesquely murdered, the looks on their faces all expressing surprise and fear.

General Montgomery's secretary sat spread-eagled on her typing chair, her arms flung back, her head hanging backward from her body, supported by only a few strands of flesh. The general himself had been shot through the abdomen, with an automatic rifle. A thick trail of blood and ripped intestines led from near the door to his desk, where the telephone he had used for his final message dangled from its cord.

Remo picked up the phone and dialed the seven-digit code number to Smith and waited for the routing connections.

"Yes," Smith said very quietly, sounding more shaken than Remo could remember ever hearing the vinegar-blooded New Englander.

"There's been a bloodbath at Fort Wheeler," Remo said. "Mostly officers. They're all dead. Nobody else seems to be around."

There was a pause at the other end of the phone. "I was afraid of that," Smith said. "The same thing has happened at the other bases where the disappearances have taken place. The pattern's been continued. It's madness."

"I may have a lead, Smitty. What's the name Vadassar mean to you?"

"Vadassar? Let me check." Remo heard the click

of buttons and the electronic garble of Folcroft's immense computer hookup in action. Then silence. "Nothing," Smith said. "Vadassar, you said? Let me try variations on the spelling."

More buttons. More silence. "No. It doesn't compute."

"That's funny. A general here who was murdered today called me before he died. The last thing he said was 'Vadassar.' "

"Maybe it's an anagram. I'll work on it. Meanwhile, there's nothing left for you to do there. Get over to Fort Borgoyne. If this horror is spreading, it'll strike there next. And hurry. This is monumentally important."

For an instant, Remo remembered the legend in his dream. *A monumental force from the West will seek to destroy Shiva.*

"Remo? Are you there?"

"I'll take care of it, Smitty," he said, and hung up.

As he looked back over the body of General Arlington Montgomery, he felt a twinge of guilt coming from deep inside him. He had been with a woman when the massacre had taken place.

There were two places he had to go before leaving for Texas. The first was locked, and Remo knew instinctively as he tried the door to her house that Randy Nooner was gone for good. He forced his fingers into the lock and shattered it from inside, then walked immediately to her bedroom closet. It was empty.

He returned to the base and followed the heavily worn trail to find the other place, the location of the evangelist Randy Nooner had mentioned.

It was deserted. In the center of the worn area

67

was a large space, excessively used, which Remo assumed had been the site for the services. He combed the area carefully with his feet, feeling with his toes for anything that may have been left behind.

There was nothing. Whoever had been at the spot had been careful to clean up before leaving. Too careful. Then he found it. He didn't see it at first, hidden under some sawdust shavings, but he could smell it. The odor of human blood was as potent to him as the scent of heavy perfume in a small room.

He scratched away the top layer of sawdust and found the dried brown smear beneath.

In the desert hundreds of miles away, a photograph of the massacre shimmied to clarity in a darkroom developing pan.

"Beautiful," a heavily accented voice said. "His Highness will like this very much. Very much indeed."

The woman developing the pictures dried her hands and turned on the light. "And Vadassar is at last a reality," said Randy Nooner.

Six

In the back of the customized sky-blue Airstream trailer, which was painted with fluffy white clouds, Samantha counted money.

"A hundred eighty-six thousand and change," she said, planting a noisy kiss on the wad of bills. "Three months out of Pontusket, and we're rich as thieves. How about that, Artie, honey?"

"It's all right, I guess," Artemis Thwill said. He gulped down a martini.

"Can't you work up any more enthusiasm than that?"

Artemis poured himself another drink.

"Quit swilling those things. This is the greatest thing that's ever happened to us, and you're turning into a lush. What kind of god are you, anyhow?"

"Get off my back," Thwill said. He tossed down the contents of the glass. "It's not easy being God."

"I just can't figure you out, Artemis," Samantha said. "Back in Iowa, when we were stomping around those one-horse towns, living on beans and mugging bums, you were happy as a pig in shit."

Artemis thought back to those early days before their marriage, when he and Samantha had set up their tent in sleepy Iowa towns and not many people had come to hear him speak. The people who did come were loose-in-the-head fanatics without a cause, mostly, or drifters looking for a place to spend a few hours out of the noonday heat.

It had been easy then. Sometimes the victims virtually offered themselves up to Artemis, hanging around in the tent after the services were over to have a private word with him. And even if they didn't, it was a simple matter to ask a few townies to linger after the rest had gone. Then he would ask them some questions about themselves, nice and neighborly, and sooner or later he'd find someone who didn't have a wife or kids or girlfriend waiting for him back home, someone who wouldn't be missed right away, and Artemis would single that person out as his special friend. Samantha would cook dinner in the Airstream for Artemis and his new special friend, and they'd all enjoy a little dinner chitchat. On these occasions Artemis's appetite would be boundless, his charm devastating, his humor infectious. Then for dessert, right along with the coffee, Artemis would land a flying right hook into his special friend's throat, or bounce his special friend's skull against a rock, or instigate an impromptu game of mumblety-peg on his special friend's torso.

Artemis sighed in remembrance. No, they didn't have two nickels to rub together back then, but those were the happiest days of Artemis Thwill's life. "Money isn't everything," he said quietly. Oh, for just one more special friend to kill. He poured himself another drink, emptying the gin bottle.

Samantha chattered on, oblivious to his reverie. "Well, don't say you didn't jump at the chance to take on this opportunity with the military."

70

"Opportunity. Crap. This army nonsense is a pile of crap."

"It's not crap. It's a splendid opportunity," Samantha pouted.

"Quit trying to sound like Randy Nooner."

"If it wasn't for Randy giving us this chance, we'd still be starving in Iowa. And you'd be heading for the hoosegow before long. Murders get to be traceable after a while, if it turns into a constant thing like it did with you. You're an addict."

"I was just having a little fun."

"You were doing in three and four guys a day, Artie."

"Nag, nag, nag," Artemis said, waving his glass in front of him. "Marry a woman and she turns into a bitch. I'll tell you what's wrong. It's that Nooner bitch, that's what. Ever since she came into the picture, all the good times went poof. Now it's just gripe, nag, moan—"

"This is a business, Artemis. And for the first time since we started, this business is making money." Her eyes were pinched and hard.

"But what about me?" Artemis yelled. "What about my *feelings*? How do you think I feel not even being allowed to write my own speeches anymore? And that pap I have to say, all that morbid stuff about carrying on after I'm with the dear departed. It gives me the willies."

"All saviors have to be martyrs, stupid," Samantha said. "That's just so that when you kick off, we can make a big deal out of it."

"For your information, Samantha, I do not intend to die just so Randy Nooner can get some good press." He drained his glass with a shudder.

"You could get hit by a bus," Samantha offered.

"And that's another thing. All the killing. It bothers me."

Samantha laughed. "Changed your tune, I guess. You used to love it."

"Yeah, before you and Randy Nooner decided to take over my life. Now I just stand around twiddling my thumbs while those dunderheaded soldiers get in all the good shots."

"Oh, Artie. They were only a few dippy chaplains who never put up much of a fight anyway. Besides," she said, imitating Randy Nooner, "it's good P.R. once the recruits are in on a kill, they're with us all the way."

"I don't give a hot shit if they're with us or not," Artemis said. "All I ever wanted was to push somebody off a bridge once in a while, or to blow some nobody's brains out." His eyes grew watery with sentiment, remembering the good old times. "I never asked for much, Samantha. A dislocated jaw here, a snapped neck there. Now what do I get for all the hours of hard work I put in, all the traveling and missed meals? A fat nothing, that's what. I can't even punch out a drunk anymore, because, according to Randy Nooner, God doesn't do that." Artemis blew his nose with a pitiful roar.

In a few minutes the Airstream and the flatbed truck behind it, which was carrying the tent and supplies, pulled off on the side of the road.

"Come on," Samantha said, stuffing the bills back into the strongbox and locking it. "Here's where we make our connection."

Artemis shambled to his feet, weaving slightly. "Just another town along the highway, another crowd of strangers," he lamented, holding back his tears.

"Quiet down," Samantha said, gingerly picking up the strongbox. "Here comes somebody."

A short, swarthy man sausaged into a lieutenant's uniform entered the trailer.

"Ah. A worshipper," Artemis said. "At least the soldiers treat me with respect. They don't nag me. To them, I'm God."

"Move it, turkey," the lieutenant said to Artemis. His words were thickly accented, and his breath gusted clouds of curry and kibbe.

"What kind of soldier are you?" Artemis demanded, letting the edge in his voice show that he didn't approve of rudeness toward his person. The lieutenant slapped him across the face and spewed out a stream of guttural foreign-sounding words.

Outside, a black Lincoln limousine waited. As the lieutenant pushed Artemis and Samantha out onto the roadway, he squeezed one of Samantha's breasts energetically, expressing his delight in a high-pitched giggle.

"Now wait a minute," Artemis said. "You can't treat my wife this way."

"My apologies, O divine Artemis," the officer said, still chuckling. He bowed in mock obedience, withdrawing a billy club from his belt as he did. He whirled the club in his hand before bringing it forward with a crack on Artemis's kneecaps. Thwill buckled under the pain and sank to the ground.

"Get in," the lieutenant commanded. He opened the door to the limo and roughly pushed Artemis inside. "At Vadassar you are not God, white-skinned imperialist American," the officer spat. He slammed the door.

In the corner of the back seat, Randy Nooner

looked up from her newspaper. "Nice trip?" she asked.

"Did you see what your driver did to me?" Thwill asked, gesturing toward the lieutenant in the front seat.

Randy pushed a button and the locks on the doors clamped shut. "You probably irritated him." From the front seat came a stream of angry, incomprehensible monologue. "Drive," she said, and slammed the partition between the front and back seats. They sped off into the night.

"How can that man be an officer in the United States Army?" Artemis continued. "He hardly speaks English."

Randy Nooner jabbed Artemis in the knee, sending sparks of pain blazing up his leg. "I'd say he gets his message across," she said. "Besides, there are more like him where we're going."

"Where's that? Dante's Inferno?"

"I thought you'd never ask." She tossed him the newspaper in her lap. On the front page was a photograph of the bloodied grounds at Fort Wheeler with the banner headline: UNEXPLAINED MASSACRES AT ARMY BASES.

"What do you think?" she asked.

Artemis gazed at the wirephoto for a long moment before realizing that a thin stream of saliva had dribbled down his chin. "It's beautiful," he said.

"Magnificent. All those recruits you've been preaching to at Fort Antwerth, Fort Beson, Fort Tannehill, and Fort Wheeler held a little revolution today. They've killed the officers and deserted the bases."

Artemis pointed to the story. "It says here that it happened at all four bases at the same time."

"We had recruits of our own planted to time the whole operation. An ingenious coup, don't you think?" She went on without waiting for an answer. "Now all the deserters are in one place, waiting for you to appear."

"Where's that?"

She spoke her words reverently. "The culmination of all our efforts. The beginning of a new army, Fort Vadassar."

"You mean the place that I've been telling those zombie soldiers all these months is the Promised Land? *That* Vadassar? A *fort?*"

Randy smiled. The limo rolled over mile after mile of highway and onto a series of dirt roads leading deep into the Texas heartland.

"I thought you made that name up. I didn't know there was a real Vadassar," Artemis said.

Randy smiled. "Of course not, dear. It didn't exist until today. Originally, Vadassar was private property, built by private funds."

"Whose?"

Randy smiled. "Don't ask so many questions, Art. You'll live longer."

They drove in silence the rest of the way.

Fort Vadassar was a miracle of modern engineering, gleaming under its acres of electric lighting like a star in the Texas wasteland. Its pristine buildings were magnificently designed with solar panels. Its grounds were lush, with oases around deep lagoons that were carved into the dry earth and irrigated by underwater pipes. On the banks around the lagoons sprouted wild tropical flowers. In the recreation compound, an Olympic-sized swimming pool shim-

75

mered in the moonlight, next to a row of perfectly kept tennis courts and a football stadium.

"Holy Moses," Samantha said. She shook Artemis awake. "Get up, Artie. Look at this."

Artemis's eyes rolled groggily. "Wha—we there?" He spotted the tennis courts and the pool. "Where the hell are we?"

"Vadassar," Randy Nooner said breathlessly. "The headquarters for the new army of the United States of America."

The car pulled in noiselessly beside a smallish ultra-modern building constructed from steel and mirrored glass. "These are the guest quarters, where you'll be staying," Randy said.

"How long?" Artemis asked warily.

"Well, let's see." Randy ticked off the agenda on her fingers. "First, there's the address to the troops. Then tomorrow we're holding a press conference—"

"I thought you said nobody knew this place existed."

"No," she said. "I didn't say that. I said Fort Vadassar didn't exist. It still doesn't, in fact. It won't exist officially for another four hours or so."

"How do you arrange that?" Samantha asked eagerly.

Randy chucked her under the chin. "I already told your husband not to ask so many questions. It's bad for your face, honey."

"You mean, like, I'll get pimples?"

Randy nodded. "And scars," she said cordially. She led them to the house, past the corporal assigned to guard the entrance. The soldier stared blankly ahead of him, chanting, "Hail Artemis," as they passed.

"Hey, I don't think I like your threats," Artemis said to Randy Nooner.

"Hail Artemis," said the guard.

"I don't care if you like them or not," Randy said.

"Hail Artemis," said the guard.

"Oh, will you shut up?"

"Hail Artemis," said the guard.

"Drop dead, Corporal," Artemis raged.

Immediately the soldier put his hands around his own throat and squeezed until the color in his face changed from white to red to purple to blue. When his eyes were bulging and his tongue lolled darkly out of his mouth, the soldier collapsed in front of Artemis.

Samantha screamed. "What the hell did he do that for?" Artemis asked.

"You told him to drop dead, didn't you?"

"I asked him to shut up first."

"But you ordered him to drop dead. These men only respond to direct orders," Randy explained.

Artemis whistled low. "Because they love me," he said.

"It's not exactly you. Lehammet, bring me another foot soldier." The swarthy lieutenant rambled off without acknowledgement. In a few minutes he returned with a private in uniform.

Artemis checked his watch. "It's almost four A.M.," he said. "Aren't these men supposed to be asleep?"

"They sleep when we tell them to." Randy turned to the young soldier. "Private, eat dirt."

The soldier dropped to his knees and began stuffing handfuls of earth into his mouth. "Go on, tell him to do something."

Samantha giggled. "Can I really?"

Randy nodded. "Okay," Samantha said with a shrug. "Drop your pants."

The private obeyed. "Jesus Christ," Artemis said. "What've you done to them?"

"You and Samantha helped," Randy said cheerfully. "You got them to set aside their own personalities for the good of the idea. All great speakers have that power. And since I wrote your speeches, their ideal was my ideal—Vadassar. Of course, Samantha's stone pony cocktails helped get the men's minds in a receptive state."

"It was nothing," Samantha said modestly. "Just apple juice laced with PCP and a little acid. I used to mix it up for parties back in junior high. One drink and your brains turn into scrambled eggs. A real blast."

"The men loved it, darling," Randy said. "After you held your communions, the men were so highly suggestible that all you had to do to turn them to violence was to bring in a victim and turn the men loose. They were like a pack of mad dogs at that stage."

"Why'd you pick chaplains to be the victims?"

Randy laughed. "Because they're the only ones who would come alone and unarmed, idiot. We didn't want the men to fail on their first kill. If they did, they might never have had the confidence to exterminate the officers at their bases today and come here."

She turned to the blank-faced soldier standing at attention in his shorts. "Go back to your barracks, private," Randy said. The private padded back where he had come from, his trousers draped around his ankles.

"He didn't even pull up his pants," Artemis noticed.

"That's because we didn't tell him to."

"Do you mean that these soldiers only do what they're told—by whoever tells them?"

The oily-looking lieutenant grinned. "That is correct, Artemis Thwill. You are not the only one who commands them now. We no longer need you."

"That's enough, Lieutenant," Randy snapped. The officer sniggered contemptuously at her command, but remained silent.

"Unfortunately, the process isn't complete yet," Randy explained. "The drugs and the first kill sent the men into a state of utter confusion. But in all four test bases, that stage ended quickly, within a couple of days. Then the men turned into automatons, like the private who was just here. At the moment, they'll take commands from anyone."

"I guess that could be dangerous," Artemis said. "In combat, all the enemy would have to do would be to order them to stop."

"Exactly. But we're training them now to respond only to us. They'll be perfect in a few days."

"Who's 'us'?" Artemis asked.

"Never mind. Go inside and get ready. You're addressing the troops in ten minutes. I've got your speech right here, so just get into your clothes." She pushed the couple into the door, closing it behind them, and kicked the corpse of the corporal who had strangled himself on Artemis's command. "Get this carcass out of here," she told the lieutenant.

"I am not one of your zombies," the lieutenant said scornfully. "I am of the true army of Vadassar, and I accept orders only from General Elalhassein."

"And General Elalhassein accepts orders from

me," she said coldly. "Now drag this body into those bushes if you want to see another sunrise."

Grudgingly, the lieutenant complied. With the corporal's remains concealed, he stomped out of the bushes. "It is done," he said sullenly.

"Show me where you put him," Randy insisted.

With a sigh of disgust, Lieutenant Lehammet led her to the spot, gesturing to the dead soldier with a courtly bow. "Are you satisfied?" he asked.

"Not quite." She reached into her purse, pulled out a .38 Smith and Wesson, and fired two shots directly into the lieutenant's brain. As his body slumped lifelessly over that of the corporal, Randy Nooner said, "Now I'm satisfied."

The huge stadium, built to accommodate 100,000 people, was only partially filled with the current population of Fort Vadassar, but the recruits present gave Artemis a full measure of divine respect. Six thousand recruits greeted him with salutes as he stumbled onto the podium, then fell to their knees in holy worship. "Hail Artemis," they rumbled.

Artemis covered the microphone and turned to Randy and Samantha, who were standing behind him. "I'm used to playing to a full house," he said.

Randy sighed. "It'll be full tomorrow, and every day after that. "Just read the speech, okay?"

He cleared his throat and unfolded the speech Randy Nooner had written for him.

"Artemis is greatly pleased with his welcome at Fort Vadassar, by the vanguard of the new army," he began.

The recruits cheered.

Artemis squinted. The thought crossed his mind

that he would soon require reading glasses. And he really should have looked over the speech before delivering it. God didn't trip over his messages to the flock, after all.

"I am come to bless your great endeavor," he read quickly, trying to sound spontaneous, "for . . ." He halted as he read the following words silently. A lone voice in the crowd filled the short silence by shouting, "Hail Artemis."

". . . For I will not be among you much longer?" he asked Randy Nooner, forgetting to cover the mike. A roar of outraged disbelief rose from the stadium. "What is this bullshit?"

"Go on, read," Randy whispered, shoving him back toward the podium.

"My mortal life is nearing its end?" he continued, still questioning the contents of his strange speech.

Screams of "No!" and "O divinity" rang out above the rumble of the troops.

"Even as I stand before you, a—what?—a government plot has been put in motion to halt my words forever. . . . Aw, come on, Nooner," he said, slapping his hand on the lectern in disgust, but his words were obliterated by the rising hysteria of the worshippers, who had just been informed that they were losing their messiah.

"Hold it," Artemis yelled, waving his arms to try to quiet the crowd. "Big mistake. Keep your pants on, everybody."

But even as he spoke, a long-nailed hand holding a hyprodermic syringe moved swiftly toward Artemis's spine, and in a moment he lay in a heap on the podium while 6,000 soldiers wailed as though the world had ended.

Seven

It was 4:50 A.M. when Jay Miller stepped into the spacious entranceway to the United States Senate building in Washington, D.C. His heart was pumping overtime, as it had since the telephone call an hour before, requesting his presence at a special breakfast meeting.

His two years in Washington had taught him not to question the summons from above. If Senator Osgood Nooner felt like having breakfast at 5:00 A.M. with the Assistant to the Chief Clerk of Records, then, by golly, Jay Miller was not about to turn down the invitation. He felt a small rush of power as he flashed his identification card to the guard inside the portals, knowing that the name Jay Miller was on the guard's list of persons who were to be allowed admittance at that hour.

"Yes, sir," the guard had said as he handed Miller a special pass.

Sir. At 26, he'd never been called "sir" in his life. He wound his way around the hallowed labyrinthine corridors, showing his special pass proudly, until he reached the office of Senator Osgood Nooner. It was guarded by a six-foot Marine who examined his

82

pass and escorted him to the senator's inner sanctum before returning to his post.

The senator was sitting at his desk, writing. Jay Miller stood in the doorway for several seconds, afraid to enter. Finally, he cleared his throat in announcement.

The senator looked up. "Ah, come in," Senator Nooner said, smiling broadly. Miller took a couple of halting steps forward as the senator rose and strode briskly toward him. "Glad you could make it, son. Hungry?"

Miller gulped. "No, sir. I mean, yes, sir."

"No need to be nervous, son," the senator said, patting Miller on the back. "We're all just ordinary people, living together in the crazy world for better or worse, right? Here, have a seat."

Miller attempted a smile as he sat down at the small table set for two with gleaming silver chafing dishes and a single red rose.

"Hope it's not too early for you, ah—"

"Miller, sir. Joshua Miller. My friends call me Jay."

The senator spooned a portion of scrambled eggs onto Miller's plate. "Jay it is, then," he said. "I'd like you to consider me your friend. Call me Ozzie."

"Yes sir, Ozzie, sir," Miller said, choking on his first bite.

The senator sat back and waited for his guest's coughing fit to subside before speaking again. "Now, Jay, you may be wondering why I invited you here. Go on, eat."

Miller obeyed, stuffing more eggs into his still-sputtering mouth.

"The fact is, Jay, I want to ask you for a favor."

"Me?" A crumb of scrambled egg flew from Miller's lips, hitting the senator square in the eye. The young man leaped up immediately, knocking over an orange juice glass and causing the table to shake precariously.

"Sit down, damn it," the senator roared, holding the sides of the table to steady it. With his napkin, he removed the offending particle, then threw the napkin onto the table with a loud slap. "Cretinous fool," he muttered before composing his face into a mask of cordiality. "That is, everything all right, Jay?"

Miller nodded. His teeth were chattering.

"What I called you in to discuss is a matter of extreme national importance, Jay, so I'd like your word that what passes between us will go no further."

"Oh, you have my absolute word on that, Ozzie, sir."

"Good. I'll get right to the point, Jay. It's the army records."

Jay Miller felt his palms begin to sweat. He was in charge of filing the records for the army in the Pentagon. "Is something wrong, sir?"

"Ozzie," the senator corrected, smiling. "Yes. Something is definitely wrong." He gave Jay's trembling hand a fatherly squeeze. "Don't worry, son. It's not your fault. The red tape in the Pentagon is—well, you know how it is." The senator chuckled and exchanged with Miller a between-us-insiders smile. "The point is, there's a whole army base in Texas that's been operating since 1979 that there aren't any records for. No construction payment records, no files on operating expenses, no personnel records, salary documentation, nothing." He laughed jovially. "Now, isn't that something?"

Jay Miller blanched. "But—but that can't be," he stammered. "If it's been operating since 1979, then surely—"

"There are no records," Senator Nooner said slowly, enunciating every word so that the idiot sitting across from him would be sure to understand.

"No, sir. There are no records," agreed Jay Miller.

"You're a smart boy, son. I think someone as bright as you is a real asset to our country. I think that a person with your brains ought to have a better job than Assistant to the Chief Clerk of Records. Don't you, Jay?"

"I—I don't know, sir."

"Call me Ozzie."

"I guess I'd like another job, sir—Ozzie. I never really thought about it."

"A job such as, say, Secretary of the Treasury?"

"Abba—abbaba," said Jay Miller.

"I'm a powerful man, son. I could arrange it."

"Abbaba—baba—"

"Excellent. I'll set the wheels in motion today. Of course, you'll have to straighten out the army files before you leave. Create new dossiers on Fort Vadassar—that's the new base—transfer the personnel files, details like that."

"Sure," Miller said, his face flushed with anticipation. "Once I get the okay, I think I can have everything in order in six weeks, Ozzie."

"You have the okay, as of now. And you've got one hour."

"One hour? But I don't even have the information to file."

Nooner smiled grandly. "That's a detail I've already taken care of, son. They don't call me the

People's Senator for nothing." He handed Miller a stack of official forms and a lengthy list of names. "Just put these in the Vadassar file bank, and transfer the personnel dossiers for the soldiers on the list from whatever camp they're in—mistakenly—to the Vadassar files. That clear?"

The young man took the papers uncertainly. "I guess so. But one hour—"

"Secretary of the Treasury," Nooner said.

"One hour it is, Ozzie."

"Good. Come back when you're through." Nooner rose to shake the young man's hand and waited for the door to close behind Jay Miller before picking up the telephone. He dialed the number of the *Washington Post*.

"This is Senator Osgood Nooner," he said. "I've just received some shocking news from an extremely reliable source about the massacres at the army bases yesterday. The word is that the Pentagon itself is responsible. The leadership at one base, Fort Vadassar, knows the story and is sufficiently outraged by its moral implications to inform the press about it in an open conference at twelve noon today."

He repeated the message, along with directions to Fort Vadassar, to the *New York Times*, the *New York Daily News*, the *Chicago Tribune*, the *Los Angeles Times*, the *Dallas Herald*, ABC, CBS, and NBC. It took him just under one hour. Then he lit a cigar and waited for the return of Jay Miller, the man who thought an assistant clerk of records could become Secretary of the Treasury by rearranging a few files.

The young man returned exactly on time, his smile indicating he had completed the job.

"Very fine work, son," Nooner said, opening the

86

desk drawer where he kept some personal effects. "Did anyone in the Pentagon's file offices try to stop you?"

"Oh, no, Ozzie," the young man said. "No one was even there at this hour, and the guards all know I run those files." He flushed with pride. "I really appreciate this opportunity, sir. I never thought I'd get a chance to work with Senator Osgood Nooner."

"I always like to give a smart fellow like you a helping hand, son," the senator said as he slipped a handkerchief over the barrel of the new, unloaded .45 automatic in the desk drawer and tossed it toward the young man. Before Miller could recognize what the flying object was, he reached out and caught it. And at the precise moment when Miller began smearing his fingerprints over the empty weapon, Senator Osgood Nooner tucked the handkerchief into his coat pocket and screamed, "Help! There's a killer in here!"

Within seconds the Marine guard stationed outside Nooner's door was in the office, his weapon drawn.

"Shoot! " Nooner yelled.

Jay Miller looked, bewildered, from the gun in his hand to the senator who had promised him a cabinet position only an hour before. And he understood, during the infinitesimal moment between the time when the guard's pistol fired and the searing, burning pain in his back obliterated every working part of his organism, that Senator Osgood "Ozzie" Nooner had spoken the truth.

There was indeed a killer present.

Eight

Remo vaulted the wire fence surrounding Fort Borgoyne, then waited while Chiun ripped the links apart and stepped through the opening. They walked to the center of the camp and slipped unnoticed into a group of new recruits stepping off the arrival bus at the parade grounds.

Remo remembered the frightened recruits of his early army days, but this was a totally different kind of crew, obviously used to standing in lines, apparently in prison mess halls, and to milling around aimlessly, presumably while employed in federal job programs.

"This is your army?" Chiun said.

"It's supposed to be."

"God save the Republic," Chiun said. "Where is the marching? Where are the banners? The cymbals?"

"This is the American army," Remo said. "Most of these guys will have to reenlist to have enough time to tell left foot from right foot."

He looked with Chiun toward an onrushing sergeant whose face suggested that his father had been a bull terrier.

"I am Sergeant Hayes, and this is the United

States Army," the sergeant boomed. "You came here to work, and work you will. Do all your orders read Fort Borgoyne?"

Only a few voices squeaked an answer. "Yes." The other enlistees seemingly did not care what their orders read, just so long as it was not Sing Sing.

"Yes what?" the sergeant yelled at the top of his lungs, although he stood no more than two feet from the ragged line of recruits.

"Yes, *sir*," a few answered in unison.

"What?"

"Yes, sir," they thundered.

"Again."

"*Yes, sir!*"

Chiun was clapping his hands together in rhythm and smiling delightedly. "Yes, sir," he squealed, marching in his own little circle. "Yes, sir! This is the real army. Yes, sir."

He turned excitedly to Remo. "You were right," he said, his long robes billowing as he stomped in single formation. "One two," Chiun called out. "Hup, tup, Wing Ho."

"Wing Ho?"

"It is an advanced drill used in the Chinese Third Dynasty. No one talks about it now, but the Chinese could never fight as well as a field of butterflies. Still, their marching was unparalleled. Kwo Hun Wing Ho."

The sergeant noticed that his new group of inductees was staring at the aged Oriental, who was marching and chanting the strange words.

"At ease," he called. Chiun continued marching. "I said cut it out, Grampa," the sergeant bellowed.

"I'd leave off the grampa stuff if I were you," Remo advised.

"Who asked you?"

Remo shrugged. "Just trying to do my bit. If you don't care about hanging onto your arms and legs, then be my guest." He made way for the sergeant to approach Chiun.

"I'll take care of you later, punk," the sergeant said, placing his hands on his hips. "What in the hell do you think you're doing here?" he demanded of Chiun.

"Is this not a training camp?"

"That's just what it is, old man."

"Very well. Remo is here to join your army, and I am his trainer."

"We got no room for nursemaids around here, Papa-san." The sergeant took another step forward so that his beefy head hovered a full two feet over Chiun's, casting a menacing shadow.

"Step back, cow-eater," Chiun warned. "You are obstructing my view."

"Obstruc—look, mister," the sergeant began, poking a stubby finger toward the old man's shoulder.

"Shouldn't have done that," Remo said as the sergeant spiraled skyward and came to rest in the branches of a cottonwood tree.

"Did you see that?" one of the recruits asked.

"Naw. Must be the heat." Remo directed the group toward another officer. "We need uniforms and supplies, Major," he said.

The major looked surprised. "What happened to your instructor?" he asked.

Remo glanced back to the tree where Sergeant Hayes was just beginning to show small signs of life. "Dunno," Remo said. "I guess he got hung up."

"Well, the supplies are in that building over

there. I'll have a sergeant meet you and take you to your quarters. Meanwhile, you're in charge." He patted Remo on the back. "You're going to make a fine soldier," he said, and walked away.

"You!" Chiun sputtered. "How can he say that you will make a fine soldier? Did you know the Third Dynasty War March? Did you engage in deadly combat with the piglet in the tree?"

"No, Little Father," Remo said, leading the group toward the supply building.

"Your army is racist and ungrateful. Never will I teach these worthless things the Wing Ho formation."

"Serves 'em right," Remo said.

Another sergeant met them at the supply office and escorted the men to their barracks, where he taught them how to make a bunk. He seemed to believe that an army traveled on its bed, and tight beds good armies made.

"Now, I want these here corners tight, y'hear?" the sergeant drawled, crisply tucking in the last corner of blanket. "That's tight, and I mean so tight a quarter bounces off it." He pronounced the word "corder." Flipping a coin from his pocket, he demonstrated. The quarter bounced a good three inches upward, after hitting the blanket.

"Now you do it," he said to Remo. With one hand he lifted the sheets and blanket off the bunk so that they lay in a crumbled heap.

"Ah, very interesting," Chiun said. "In your army, you make the bed, then you unmake it. Then you make it again. Very Zen. Also I see now what you do to be designated a fine soldier, Remo. I knew you must be extraordinarily talented in some area, since you do not march or engage in combat.

91

Now I see that your worthy event is bedmaking. Highly appropriate, Remo."

"Lay off," Remo said.

"What was that?" the sergeant roared.

"Nothing. And I can hear you, so stop yelling." He began to smooth the bedding over the bunk.

"Oh, wise guy, huh?"

Remo sighed. The scenario was becoming more and more reminiscent of the early days of his two-year stint in the army. Maybe sergeants never changed. The thought occurred to him that it would take a lot of self-control to make it through even one day of boot camp.

"Tuck in that corner, dogface," the sergeant demanded.

"Dogface?" Chiun brightened at the word. "What an apt description." He tittered, repeating the word *dogface* over and over, as though it were the most hilarious thing he'd heard all day. "Dogface Remo. Hah. Dogface. Heh, heh."

"And if I want any lip from you, old timer, I'll ask for it."

Chiun's mirth vanished.

"Just go along, Chiun," Remo said. "If we're going to find anything out, we can't kill everybody here."

"What's that you're mumbling, smartass?"

"Nothing."

"Nothing, *sir*," the sergeant corrected.

"Don't stand on formality, Sarge," Remo said.

The sergeant glared at Remo with eyes as cold as the teats of a 50-year-old WAC. "Something tells me you ain't going to work out, mister," he said threateningly. Then his face broke into a malevolent grin. "But I'm a fair man. Tell you what I'm going to do. If you make this bunk right, we'll start off with a clean slate. But if a quarter don't bounce one foot off the bed, you and the old Jap are going to the hotbox." He laughed. He had witnessed too many barracks bets not to know that a quarter would not bounce more than five inches.

"Jap?" Chiun gasped. "Now, this is too much. Calling you a dogface is one thing, but referring to the Master of Sinanju as a Japanese—"

"Shhh. Just go along."

"Go along, he says. Always go along. No matter that the glory of Sinanju has been tarnished. No matter that my weary being has been encircled with shame."

"Here's the quarter," the sergeant said, smiling cruelly. "And if it don't bounce twelve inches off this bunk, you get the hotbox. Got it?"

"Yup," Remo said. He took the quarter and tossed it on the bed, where the coin made a small dent before flying upward with a *whoosh* and embedding itself in the ceiling.

The eyes of every man in the barracks were fixed on the metal disk. "How'd you do that?" the sergeant asked.

"Just lucky, I guess. Looks like the hotbox'll have to wait."

The sergeant's face reddened. "Like hell, you cheatin' Yankee," he said. He reached out to grab Remo's arm.

"Just go along," Chiun said sagely. But Remo's reflexes were trained to respond automatically to assault, and to Remo's nervous system, the sergeant's sweaty grip constituted assault. Before the stubby

93

fingers completed their circle around Remo's wrist, they were numb, and the sergeant was gripping his forearm where Remo's thumb had bruised it.

Then one of the recruits clapped Remo on the shoulder and said, "Attaboy, bro. Time somebody hit that sucker," and Remo knew he had made a mistake.

"Which way to the hotbox?" he asked the sergeant, who was writhing in pain beside Remo's bunk. "I'm going to turn myself in."

"Huh?" the recruit asked. "What you doing that for? You just showed that mother who's running things around here."

"America is running things around here," Remo said. "And when you join the army, you do things the army way. I was wrong, and I'm going to pay the penalty. C'mon, Chiun."

"Chickenshit," the recruit called to Remo's back. Remo flicked out his hand toward the recruit's nose, grabbed it, and squeezed. The recruit quickly changed his mind. "Over there," he began to sing, twanging nasally and tapping his foot.

"That's better." Remo led Chiun in silence to the small corrugated metal building on the edge of the camp. He told the guard that he had been told to report to the hotbox. The guard shrugged and waved him inside.

Chiun wrinkled his nose at the scent of the sweating inmates who lined the walls. "Why, may I ask, did you volunteer us for incarceration in this pit?" he asked.

"We were setting a bad example, Chiun. Nobody likes being at boot camp, but if every recruit just wasted whoever was in charge of making a soldier out of him, we wouldn't have an army. We'd have what happened back at Fort Wheeler."

"I see. And by imprisoning ourselves, we will make better soldiers out of the others."

"Something like that." He turned to address one of the soldiers in the hotbox. "Say, do you know anything about some religious group coming around here?"

"Whaddya want, jerk?" the soldier snarled. "I don't know nothing about no religious crap, so how's about shutting your face. Unless you got some smoke."

"Then again, we could break out of this stinkhole whenever we wanted," Remo said to Chiun.

"That is reassuring," Chiun said, and sent the soldier crashing through the wall, over the fence, and deep into the woods beyond. Chiun hurried the other prisoners along the same route until he and Remo were alone in the cell. "This room was badly in need of proper ventilation," Chiun said, positioning himself lotus-style near the hole, which extended the length and breadth of the entire far wall. "Tell me when you are prepared to leave."

Remo leaned against the metal wall of the chamber. "Say, Chiun," he said, "did you notice anything odd about this place?"

"Nothing. It is filled with obnoxious white men who live down to their heritage with appalling accuracy. A perfectly ordinary community of your people."

Remo stood in silence for a moment, his brow furrowed. Finally he said, "He hasn't come here yet."

"Who? Be articulate, Remo, at least in your own language."

"The traveling preacher. Randy Nooner mentioned him, and there was blood in the place where his tent was. The guy you just threw out of here didn't know anything about any religious fanatics, and nobody at this base looks like a zombie. This is a normal army camp. It hasn't been touched by the craziness we saw at Wheeler."

"Preachers? Tents? Zombies?"

"We're in the wrong place, Chiun. The preacher's who we want. It's the preacher. We've got to find him."

"I am reasonably certain he is not in this jail," Chiun said. "If you feel you have adequately incarcerated us both to serve your country, perhaps we should seek after him elsewhere."

Just then, the door opened, and four officers entered with a crisp stamping of feet. They formed two lines to allow a man wearing a three-piece gray suit and an expression of lemony rectitude to enter. "That's the man," Harold W. Smith said, indicating Remo.

"O mighty emperor," Chiun said, according Smith a small bow. "You have heard of our plight and are come to rescue us." He leaned close to Remo and whispered, "Do not tell Emperor Smith that we could have escaped. It would lessen the kindness of his gesture."

"How'd you know we were here?" Remo asked.

"I followed your trail," Smith said blandly. From his pocket he produced a set of handcuffs. "Just go along with it," he said in a low voice, snapping the cuffs over Remo's wrists.

"I wish you'd put that another way," Remo said.

"They think you're an escaped patient from Folcroft, and that Chiun is your custodian." He cleared his throat. "Ah, the other inmates seem to have escaped, Colonel," Smith said, nodding toward the hole in the far wall.

"I see, Dr. Smith." The colonel motioned for the guard to investigate. "Is this your man's work?"

"Folcroft will pay for all damages, Colonel," Smith said. "Meanwhile, I'd better take him back. Thank you for all your help."

"Thank you, Doctor. That man would have been a serious danger here. You've wasted no time tracking him down." The colonel nodded to Smith, then to Chiun. "And your courage in trying to keep this lunatic under control is commendable."

"It is difficult, but I do what I must," Chiun said, his pride tinged with suffering. He elbowed Remo in the ribs. "Struggle," he whispered. "Act as though you are trying to free yourself from these metal bracelets." He raised his voice. "Back, beast," he shouted, slapping Remo's face. "Clear away," Chiun ordered the officers. "I will subdue the madman. Back, dogfaced one." He made a show of striking Remo again. "Go on, Remo, fight," he whispered.

Reluctantly, Remo raised his hands to cover his face. In doing so, he snapped the handcuffs in two. He tried to tie the chain together, but the metal crumbled into shards. "Where'd you get these, Smitty, Toy City?" Remo asked.

Smith escorted him wordlessly out of the compound while Chiun spun around them both, flailing at Remo and shrieking, "Back, mad white lunatic!" for the benefit of passersby.

Outside the gate, Remo let the scraps of metal remaining from the handcuffs drop to the ground.

"Submit, wildman," Chiun yelled.

"Er—thank you, Chiun," Smith said, "but we needn't continue the ruse."

The old Oriental shrugged. "The Master of Sinanju respects his emperor's wishes," he said. He turned to Remo. "But do not forget your place, dogface. Heh, heh. Dogface."

"I'll keep it in mind," said Remo. "What are you doing here, Smitty? Aren't you going out on a limb by coming after us?"

"Yes, but we haven't got any time to lose. One of our operatives at the *New York Times* came through with some information you'd better investigate right away." He told Remo about the press conference scheduled for noon at Fort Vadassar. "The *Times* checked everything out with the Pentagon files. Apparently, Vadassar's been operating since 1979."

Remo looked disgusted. "Thanks a lot, Smitty. You said you couldn't find a trace of Fort Vadassar on your computers. You could have saved me this whole trip if your information was correct."

"My information is always correct," Smith said, his face expressionless.

"Is that so. Then how do you explain an army base that's been around since 1979?"

"Given the reliability of the Folcroft information terminals, there is only one explanation possible. Vadassar does not exist."

"What about the Pentagon files?"

"They must be wrong."

Remo looked at Smith sideways. "But Smitty," he said, trying to sound reasonable, "the army's holding the conference. They ought to know if their fort exists or not."

Smith's calm remained unruffled. "I don't care if the man in the moon is holding the press conference, Remo. Fort Vadassar is not a base for the United States Army. Now you find out what it is."

Nine

Artemis Thwill awoke to the taste of bitter black coffee burning his tonsils.

"Up and at 'em, Art," Randy Nooner said. "Two hours to showtime."

Thwill tried to shake himself out of his drugged stupor. "My back," he murmured, touching the sore spot where the needle had entered. "What did you do to me?"

"Only a mild sedative. It worked wonders. The troops think the government is out to kill you. Seeing you alive will give their morale a real shot in the arm."

"Samantha," he moaned.

"I'm right here, honey," Samantha called from the floor, where she was counting a stack of greenbacks. She licked her lips in appreciation. "Golly, Artemis, that fainting spell of yours pulled in almost fifty thousand dollars. And we didn't even have a service. Maybe we should make it a regular part of the routine."

"No," Artemis said, feeling the headache throb in his skull.

Randy Nooner smiled. "No," she repeated.

"That's only for special occasions. Like when Artemis doesn't feel like reading his speeches the way they were written. You won't make that mistake again, will you, Artemis?" Her eyes grew cold as she spoke ever more softly. "Because if you do, the next shot won't be a tranquilizer. And coffee won't wake you up. Do you understand?"

The very air in the room seemed to chill with her words. For an endless moment the three figures remained motionless in the room: Thwill lying on the bed, his face blank with fear; Randy Nooner standing above him, her freezing stare radiating the truth of her words; and Samantha, sitting stock still on the rug, the money sifting through her fingers like sand.

Samantha was first to speak. "Hey, guys, how about if I brew a fresh pot of coffee?" she offered brightly.

"There isn't time," Randy Nooner said. She pulled a piece of paper from her jacket. "Here's your speech, Mr. God. Read it exactly as it's written." She walked slowly to the door, opened it, and turned around to face Artemis. "Or else be prepared to meet your co-maker." She laughed humorlessly and was gone.

The stadium at Fort Vadassar buzzed with the preparations of newsmen, camera crews, and sound technicians, interspersed with the teams of undercover FBI, CIA, and army intelligence agents sent to investigate the press conference. A cluster of reporters gathered around Senator Osgood Nooner, who had arrived a few minutes before via helicopter. Remo spotted him and joined the group.

"How are you involved in all this, Senator?" a

young man with a microphone asked, careful to keep his most photogenic side toward the television cameras.

"Son, every American interested in uncovering the heinous developments leading to the government's atrocities at Forts Antwerth, Beson, Tannehill, and Wheeler is involved. That's why you boys in the press are so vital to our country. Without you, the truth might never be known, the perpetrators of these massacres never uncovered."

"Senator, how do you know the government ordered the killings?"

Nooner looked thoughtful, posing carefully in front of each of the network cameras. "Fellow human beings," he said, "all I know is that four U.S. Army bases were attacked simultaneously and without provocation. Each of these bases was located in a remote area. There were no traces of invasion by foreign powers or domestic elements, and no aerial bombing. These are the facts. I leave it to you."

"Ladies and gentlemen," the young reporter said, stepping in front of Nooner to permit a full close-up shot of himself, "the senator has indicated that all facts point to the Pentagon's direct participation in the mystery massacres at the four army bases struck yesterday, leaving thousands dead. If the Senator's theory is true, the 'Pentagon Slaughters,' as insiders are calling yesterday's event, may prove to be the biggest and most bizarre atrocity ever perpetrated by the United States in its long history of oppression and murder. Details tonight on a special hour-long edition of 'Up the Americas.' "

"Hey," a voice called from the group.

The senator looked down distastefully at the thin man dressed in a black T-shirt and chinos. The man didn't have a TV camera trained on him, so the senator tried to dismiss him, but the T-shirted fellow was persistent. "I hear that mostly officers were killed on those bases. What happened to the rest of the men?" Remo asked.

The crowd murmured as the senator took a deep breath. Who was this nobody, he thought, and how did he know about the missing recruits? Only the army's cleanup detail knew the exact number of dead and their ranks, and no one would believe the army after today, anyway.

As Nooner worded his answer in his mind, the group of reporters around him swelled. The cameras whirred. He opted for an offensive position. "I don't know what you're talking about. Everybody knows the camps were entirely wiped out. To the last man . . . person. And if you're some kind of crank who wandered into this extremely important conference to deter these fine men and women of the press from finding the truth in this terrible perversion of liberty, then you are as guilty as the Pentagon in protecting the menace to our American way of life that that vile organization represents."

The reporters cheered. Nooner breathed a sigh of relief. But he would have the young man with the thick wrists watched.

A woman reporter wearing a hot pink dress over her lush figure jiggled her way in front of the senator. "Is it true that your daughter is one of the officers at Fort Vadassar?"

Remo's ears perked. As the senator proudly affirmed the question, Remo saw Randy Nooner in her captain's uniform at the speaker's podium, stationed between a harrassed-looking man in white robes and a dark, mustachioed general who somehow seemed as if he would be more at home on a camel than in an American army barracks. To the general's left was a string of high-ranking officers, all ethnic-looking men with skins tanned dark from lifetimes of living in blistering sun.

Remo walked closer to get a better look at the men. As he approached, Randy Nooner's face froze in recognition.

"Hiya," he said, stepping up the bleachers to the podium. "Remember me? We had a date to go to prayer meeting, but you ran off with Ali Baba and the forty thieves here." The general rumbled something in a strange language. The other officers rumbled back.

"*No comprende,* fellas," Remo said. "Back when I was in the army, we spoke English. But then I wasn't an officer."

"Remo, please. These are ranking military leaders."

"In whose army? Genghis Khan's?"

The general half closed his lizard eyes and nodded to two of his officers. As they rose, one jerked his head toward the back of the stadium.

"Excuse me, Miss Nooner," Remo said. "I think these gentlemen feel like taking a stroll."

"Oh. Of course," she said. As Remo walked away, wedged between a colonel and a major, Senator Nooner came quietly to her side.

"I saw that man with you, honey," the senator said. "I want you to be careful. He was nosing around about things he shouldn't know anything about. He might be dangerous."

Randy pinched her father's cheek playfully. "Don't worry about a thing, Daddy. He's not going to be dangerous much longer. General Elalhassein sent two of his men to take care of him for us."

"Good. Thank you, General." The senator bowed to the reptilian little man wearing the metal-encrusted general's uniform.

"In the service of our country," the general said.

"Ah, yes." The senator looked at the vast expanse of land and sky around him and breathed deeply. "Our country," he said.

Remo got only as far as the bottom step leading to the stadium's deserted back wall before the two officers pulled shiny knives out of their belts and inserted them between their teeth with the precision of Radio City Rockettes. With equally perfect timing, they each withdrew a long, curved saber and circled Remo, slashing as they moved.

"Hey, boys, over here," Remo said, dodging the saber swings so quickly that it seemed he hardly moved. "Missed again. Still, you fight better than you smell."

The slashing became more furious as the two officers moved closer together. Then, as the sabers nearly met, Remo caught both blades between his thumbs and index fingers and hurled them high in the air.

The officers gasped as they saw the lethal swords arcing gracefully over the wall of the stadium, turning, and shooting downward with increasing speed toward the section of bleachers in which the podium was built.

The major took the knife from between his teeth and, roaring something wild and ancient-sounding, lunged screaming at Remo, who waited until the man was midway through a flying leap before

105

grasping his ankles. The move was so fast that the major was still in position, stiff-armed, knife pointed straight ahead, while Remo swung him like a giant acne-scarred blackjack aimed for the other officer. The knife's blade struck the colonel's midsection at the base. With a rip, it tore through his belly, gutting him amid screams of agony as the colonel's entrails spilled like slippery red fish onto the ground.

"Didn't anyone ever tell you not to play with knives?" Remo chided the major in his arms, whose face had become a study in horror. With one finger, Remo flicked the dagger from the man's hand, then crushed his skull to the consistency of used tea bags.

Back at the podium, a crowd had assembled to marvel at the two sabers, which still quivered on either side of General Elalhassein's legs. He was blubbering and incanting singsong prayers as the other officers tried vainly to remove the swords from the wood of the bleachers. "Did I miss something?" Remo asked.

The general cast a fearful glance his way and began screaming incoherently. He was led away by the other officers.

Randy Nooner stepped from her spot on the podium, catching Remo by the arm. "How did you do that?" she asked, her voice artificially even.

"Aw shucks, ma'am. T'warn't nothing. Who's your friend?" He nodded toward Artemis, who seemed oblivious to the goings-on, immersed as he was in folding and unfolding a piece of paper in his hands.

Randy called him over. "This is Artemis Thwill, our new religious leader," she said quietly, clasping her hands tightly together to keep them from trembling. It was an activity she had begun as soon as she saw the sabers falling from the sky.

"Well, nice to meet you, Artemis. Say, you aren't the same guy who was talking to the troops at Fort Wheeler, are you?

Artemis did not respond or change his expression. The worn piece of paper in his hands folded and unfolded.

Randy Nooner looked at Artemis, then at Remo. She looked back at Artemis. Her hands stopped shaking. She smiled. Brilliantly. She had an idea. "He's the one," she said, suddenly cheerful. "I'll arrange for you to talk to him at his home after the conference. Would you like that?"

"Oh, yes I would," Remo said. "I certainly would like to meet Mr. Artemis and talk things over with him."

"Good. Artemis?" She poked at Thwill's inert figure, as he folded and refolded his speech in his hands. "Artemis!" Randy yelled.

Thwill looked up, bewildered. "What? Did you say something?"

"Remo is going to pay you a visit after the press conference. Isn't that nice? He's going to be your special friend."

"Uh huh," Artemis agreed tonelessly, resuming folding his speech.

"I said he's going to be your special friend, dumdum. Get it?" She dug her nails into his arm.

"Special . . . " His face colored as he remembered with pleasure the parade of drifters and loners whom he took to be his special friends back in the days before celebrity took his one amusement in

107

life, killing people, away from him. He recalled fondly the special friends of his past and the inventive methods by which they met their ends. "Sure," Artemis said, gratitude pouring from his heart. "My special friend. Thank you, Randy. Thank you."

Ten

In light of General Elalhassein's indisposition, Randy Nooner took the podium. "Ladies and gentlemen of the press," she said. "I stand before you now in defiance of the army which I serve. I and the other officers at Fort Vadassar do this in order to protect the men under our command from the same fate that befell those innocent soldiers at Forts Antwerth, Beson, Tannehill, and Wheeler, whose lives were snuffed out by the machinations of the United States government under the direction of the Pentagon."

Chiun shifted restlessly in his seat, grumbling. "There is not even marching in this army," he complained. "No singing, no combat, nothing. Just speeches. Talk and swimming pools. Let us go back to the other camp, Remo, the one where you are rightly considered a dangerous lunatic. That place was much more enjoyable."

"Smith wants us here."

"Talk, talk, talk," he groused. "The Quati have always been excessive talkers."

"Quati?"

"Those men who were seated here with the gold

decorations on their hats and their silly sabers. Knives, always knives with the Quati. They fear using their hands for anything more exerting than feeling melons."

"They're the ranking officers of this base," Remo said.

"Quati," Chiun insisted stubbornly. "I can still smell the stench of roasted lamb in their bellies."

Randy Nooner looked back at them angrily, demanding silence. Remo sat back smiling attentively, his arms folded in front of him.

"The first and foremost question each of you undoubtedly is asking is why," she continued. "Why would the military headquarters of our nation wish to murder its own soldiers? For this I must direct your attention to one who was well loved by those martyred soldiers, for it was out of love for him that the victims of the Pentagon's purge of the faithful were forced to give up their lives rather than forsake their savior."

She breathed deeply, allowing a stricken look to settle over her face. "He was injured yesterday by the agents of the Pentagon, who wished to silence him, but faith is stronger than death, and by a miracle, he is with us now to shed light and understanding for all peoples. Ladies and gentlemen, I present the earthly vessel of our undying faith, our beloved Artemis."

She stepped down, and the strange-looking long-haired man in white robes took her place at the podium. At the instant he appeared, the 6,000 soldiers stationed in the center of the stadium fell to their knees, bowing low and crying, "Hail Artemis!" and "A miracle!" and "Artemis lives forever!"

The throng of attendant newsmen buzzed with

110

questions and speculation. Flashbulbs popped. Camera lenses zoomed in for closeups. Teams of reporters for national news magazines whispered possible headlines to one another that were sure to boost circulation. "America's New Savior" would be boxed beside the lead story on the Pentagon Slaughters.

Artemis unfolded his carefully practiced speech and read it exactly as it was written. It was a marvel of prose, ambiguous yet insinuating. It hinted that the soldiers at the stricken camps had turned to Artemis in despair after their maltreatment at the hands of the U.S. Army. It suggested that the military bigwigs learned of the soldiers' new-found faith and regarded it as a threat to their own demands for unquestioned loyalty. It outlined in veiled terms the army's punishment of its chaplains for being powerless to contain the surge of faith directed now at Artemis. The speech did not state that Artemis was God, but left those listening to it assured that he was. It was Artemis Thwill's finest hour.

"And now the greatest fear of all men who cherish faith in their souls has come to pass," he concluded. "The secular powers have determined to obliterate the holiness inherent in all by murdering those of the faith. Even now, a government plot to . . . " His voice caught, but he forced himself to go on. ". . . To destroy me is in operation, and it will succeed."

Gasps of "No!" emanated from the stadium, not only from the recruits but even more loudly from the media representatives who were now won over by the fresh attack on the government that protected attacks on itself, even if they were unjustified and untrue.

111

"Before long, I will—I will be dead," Artemis said. "The devils who fear the strength of the faithful will wield their evil might to kill me, hoping to kill the faith that I, in my humble way, have spawned."

He paused. Now that the hard part was over with, Artemis threw himself into the last of his speech with renewed vigor. "But that faith will not die," he intoned, his voice recapturing his former zeal. "The enlightened leadership at Fort Vadassar has made this base a haven for those of the faith. And so, before the perverted military powers of this government succeed in disposing of my earthly body and bringing calumny to bear on my name, I invite all who cherish truth and the salvation of their souls to gather at Fort Vadassar as a new and independent army to forge the beginnings of a military force founded upon goodness and righteousness."

Cheers went up from the troops in the stadium, their tear-stained faces gazing up at Artemis.

"Hail Artemis," chanted the soldiers.

"Hail Artemis," shouted the reporters.

One of the younger newsmen from a midwestern daily turned to his photographer and asked, "What the hell did he say?"

The photographer pulled away from his eyepiece long enough to cast the reporter a look of profound contempt. "Stupid, he said that the Pentagon killed those guys, and that any soldier who doesn't want to get his head blown off had better get his ass over here fast."

"But that's desertion," the reporter said.

The photographer shot off another five frames of Artemis standing before his kneeling legion of troops. "Nope," he answered. "That's God."

Within an hour, news bulletins about the Pentagon Slaughters charged the air waves of every radio and television station in the country. *Time* and *Newsweek* had consulted one another about which photographs of the massacres each would use for the covers of their next editions. "Artemis" had become a household word with the media, as a symbol of hope and justice. The Pentagon was bombarded with demands that members of the Joint Chiefs of Staff appear on national television to face the charges against them. A special senate committee, to be headed by Osgood Nooner, was formed on the spot to investigate all military officials.

Members of Congress signed a petition to request that the President issue a statement about his role in the Slaughters. A special Gallup poll was devised to determine the amount of trust the average American citizen held in his government.

And already thousands of army recruits were deserting their bases for Fort Vadassar.

Remo waited for the crowd that gathered around Randy Nooner to clear away before approaching her. She was speaking to her father, who cut his own words short when he saw Remo. Senator Nooner whispered something in his daughter's ear. While he talked, she looked at Remo, laughed, and blew him a kiss.

"Don't worry, Daddy," she said reassuringly. "I'm going to take care of everything." Without acknowledging Remo, the senator left.

"I guess that's that," Randy said breathlessly, taking both Remo's and Artemis's arms in her own. "It seemed like a successful conference."

"Depends on what you want to succeed at," Remo said.

Chiun pulled up the rear, alongside Samantha. "All talk," he said.

In the guest quarters, Randy and Samantha entertained Chiun in the living room while Artemis took Remo upstairs to a plush den furnished in rich velvets and French antiques. With a rustle of his long white robes, Artemis closed the door behind them and leaned on it, triggering a lock Remo could hear even through the ample insulation of Thwill's body.

"If I really wanted to leave, I could use the window," Remo said.

Artemis smiled. "Just ensuring us a little privacy," he said, lifting a cut crystal decanter. "Care for some brandy, friend?"

"No thanks. I care to know what's going on around here."

"I don't know what you mean," Artemis said, pouring himself a snifter. He held the glass up to the light. Through the dark liquid, he saw Remo's outline and felt his old hunger rise in his throat. He wanted to leap at him that second, to press his weight onto the young man's neck and hear the satisfying crunch of breaking bones, but he restrained himself so that he might fully savor the moment when it came.

"There's something fishy about this place," Remo said.

"Oh?" Artemis sipped his brandy languidly, picturing in his mind Remo's truncated limbs spread around the floor in interesting patterns.

"There are people who don't think Vadassar existed until yesterday."

Artemis gestured expansively out the window toward the buildings on the base, the tennis courts, the swimming pool, the recruits who stood in stiff formation on the grounds, gazing at their leaders with blank, zombielike stares. "Does this look like a figment of somebody's imagination?"

"What about all the foreigners running this base?"

Artemis shrugged. "The army is an equal opportunity employer," he said. "I suppose they can make officers of anyone they choose."

"Let's put it this way. Whatever else might be strange about Fort Vadassar, it's full of runaway soldiers from the camps where the killings took place. Camps where you spoke to the troops." He was bluffing, but the look of surprise on Thwill's face confirmed Remo's guess.

"Who sent you?" Artemis asked.

"Never mind. And you just invited every soldier in the country to go AWOL and join Randy Nooner's space cadets here. I want to know why."

Artemis was silent for a long moment as he realized the effect of his speech at the press conference. "That's how she's building her army," he said slowly. "Deserters. That's what she needed me for."

"Nooner?"

"Of course. Everybody else around here either doesn't speak English or is too stoned to tie a shoelace." A small smile of resignation played bitterly on Thwill's lips. "I wish I could help you," he said, shaking his head. "You know, it didn't start out this way. I mean with me being the messiah of a new military elite and all that. I never even knew about this place until this morning. And now that my usefulness is over with, she's going to get rid of me." He raised a hand to halt any possible objections from

Remo. "Oh, I know that's what she's got in store for me. Why else would she have me constantly talking about plots to do me in?' He sighed. "It's all becoming too much for me. Sometimes I wish she'd just murder me and get it over with." He drained the last of his brandy.

"But why does Randy Nooner want to take over the army?" Remo asked.

With some effort Artemis hoisted himself from his embroidered wing chair. "That, my special friend, is the question," he said wearily.

He focused on Remo's lean figure. A twig, he thought. One good shove against a plaster wall, and those skinny ribs would pop like marimbas. A right hook to the head, and Remo's neck would twist and splinter. A couple of broken legs thrown in. A mashed nose. Good lord, real lord, he thought, how long had it been since he'd mashed a nose?

"You all right?" Remo asked, concerned about the look of frenzy that was beginning to glaze in Artemis's eyes.

"Lamb of Artemis," Thwill intoned, lumbering toward Remo. "Do not try to hide your fear. The moment of one's death is one of glory," he said, picking up speed. Remo moved to another corner of the room. Thwill followed at a trot. "Look to the Hereafter," Artemis called, tucking in his shoulder and soaring into a flying tackle. Remo ducked in time to avoid 228 pounds of lurching pork loin. Had Artemis made contact, he would have slammed Remo just below the chest cavity. As it was, however, Artemis's heave propelled him into the wall, cracking his right shoulder and showering him with dried plaster.

Stunned, Artemis dragged himself to his feet and

116

lunged again, this time head-on into a rocking chair that swung crazily for a moment before dumping Artemis with a crash onto the bar. Glass flew everywhere. A shard caught Artemis over his left eyebrow, and blood trickled down his face as he rolled shakily to the floor.

"Here, let me give you a hand," Remo said, extending his arm to Thwill.

"So you want to fight dirty, huh?" Artemis raged, slapping Remo's hand away. "We'll see who can fight dirty around here. No more mister nice guy, buddy." As he jumped to a standing position, he slipped on a pool of Jack Daniels and careened into a bookcase beside the bar. The impact of Thwill's body against the Louis XV étagère caused a shelf to break in two, toppling dozens of leather-bound volumes onto his head. They landed with thunks as Artemis staggered beneath them. "You know how to throw a punch, boy, I give you that," Thwill said.

"Look, I just want to help you up."

"Trying to trick me, are you?" Legs buckling beneath him, Artemis pulled himself up to a squat and grabbed the biggest object on the bookcase, a 2-½-foot-tall Chinese vase painted with cherry blossoms. Breathing heavily, Thwill aimed himself for Remo, the vase clutched tightly in his arms.

Remo backed away. "Mister, I'm not looking to fight with you," he said. "I just want to discuss—"

"My ass," Artemis hissed. "You're trying to kill me. Some special friend you turned out to be."

And with his final shred of strength, Artemis Thwill raised the Chinese vase over his head and lowered it fiercely in Remo's direction. Unfortunately, the window was also in Remo's direction, directly behind him, in fact, and when the vase began

117

its mighty descent downward, it was through the window, with Artemis trailing helplessly behind it and cursing Randy Nooner with his last breath. In a second, Artemis Thwill and the Chinese vase struck pavement below. Both cracked.

"Pax Vobiscum," Remo said. He snapped the lock on the door and stepped quietly into the hallway.

Samantha had heard the racket and run in from the living room, Chiun following behind. She was already screaming. "You killed him!" she shrieked. "It's clear-cut murder."

"I didn't kill him," Remo said.

"Of course you did, darling," Samantha said. "Murder. Do you know what double indemnity pays for murder?" With brisk efficiency, she pulled a sheaf of papers from a bureau drawer. "With a policy this size—"

"He killed himself," Remo said.

Suddenly Samantha's sparkling eyes grew murky and cold. "Don't you ever say that to me again," she said.

"I just wanted you to know I didn't kill your husband—"

"It better be murder, mister, or I'll follow you the rest of your miserable life."

"Okay, okay," Remo said. "Whatever makes you happy. Where's Randy Nooner?"

"Gone," Samantha said, her voice still menacing. "And you'd better take off, too, if you know what's good for you. My husband was murdered, the murderer got away, and I get double indemnity." She whirled ferociously on Chiun. "Right?"

"Of course, gracious lady," he said, nodding.

"For the sake of your double identity, Remo will be pleased to murder your husband."

"He's already been murdered," Samantha stormed.

"So much the better," Chiun said. With a bow, he followed Remo out onto the grounds of the army base in search of Randy Nooner.

Samantha reached her by telephone. "I just wanted you to know that Remo guy you brought over here is on his way to your place."

"Fine," Randy said. "I'm not at my place. Your call was transferred automatically to the car. How are you, Samantha darling?"

"I'm rich," Samantha said, barely able to contain her excitement. "Artemis is dead. Remo killed him."

There was a moment of silence, followed by peals of laughter. "Perfect," Randy gasped. "Perfect, perfect. Now our Artemis is a martyr for all time."

"And I just made a half a million dollars in insurance money," Samantha said.

"We'll drink a toast to him when I get back"

"When will that be?" Samantha asked.

Randy said something that didn't make sense to Samantha. Samantha asked her to repeat it, but Randy had already hung up. For a moment Samantha kept the dead phone to her ear, puzzling over the words she thought she had heard Randy Nooner speak. They didn't make any sense, for what she thought she had heard were the words: "When I'm queen."

Eleven

Randy Nooner's house was guarded by a solitary sentry, a young man with red hair and freckles and sky-blue eyes as vacant as space.

"Your name," he said flatly as Remo and Chiun approached.

"Call me Ishmael," Remo said.

With precise, robot movements the sentry took a small piece of paper from his pocket. On it was written the name of the man Randy Nooner had called him about from her car. He stared impassively at the name on the paper. "Spell 'Ishmael,'" he said.

"R.E.M.O."

The letters matched. "Enter," he said, stepping aside.

The moment Remo and Chiun walked over the threshold, a whistle blew, and all the exits to the house closed and locked simultaneously.

From the corner of his eye, Chiun spotted a khaki sleeve in a window. "Down," he commanded.

Remo dropped to the floor. "What the hell—"

A split second later, the open fire began. Light

120

from the blaze of a half-dozen M-16's spat through the room in a fury of destruction.

"To the blind spot in the corner," Remo whispered, nodding toward a space angled between two windows. Judging the trajectory of the bullets from the positions of the soldiers at the windows and the smoldering, jagged holes on the floor, Remo and Chiun wriggled in a quick pattern past the bursts of fire to the corner.

"We can reach the cellar door from here if we move fast," Remo said.

Arching his back like a cat's, Chiun sprang forward in a blur into the rain of bullets and out the other side. Remo met him inside the cellar door.

"Look, I thought we were just making a house call. I didn't expect the charge of the light brigade, either."

"Be silent and find a way out of this noise," Chiun shouted over the din of gunfire.

"Okey dokey," Remo said, searching for an opening in the basement walls. The only window was a small rectangle through which could be seen the legs of a soldier firing into the ground floor. Remo watched the legs quizzically. "Don't they know we're not up there anymore? They just keep shooting into an empty room."

"Perhaps you could ponder the quality of their eyesight at another time," Chiun suggested. "Get us out of here. Now. It is expremely irritating to one of my serene disposition to be subjected to this dialogue of Western weaponry. Particularly with us as the target."

"I'm looking, Little Father."

"You sing. You crash cars. You lead me into rooms full of booms. Never do I experience peace of

121

mind with you. I am but a poor innocent in the twilight of his years. When have I asked for anything more than a quiet evening made lovely by the scent of the wild rose—"

"All right, already," Remo yelled. "We'll use the window."

"Remove the person standing in front of it first."

With a sigh, Remo said, "Yes, Little Father," and etched a deep groove around the perimeter of the window with his fingernail. Then, using the tips of his fingers for suction, he pulled the glass inward without a sound.

The soldier above continued to fire into the house, oblivious to the activity by his feet until they were swept from beneath him and he felt himself being yanked at incredible speed through the small opening of the basement window. Before he could scream, Remo silenced him with a two-finger thrust to the throat.

"C'mon," Remo said. "I'll lead, in case there are more waiting outside." He pulled himself partially through the narrow opening and peeked out. Two other soldiers were at the wall, but they too were firing steadily into the house, their eyes locked on the maelstrom of bullets and dust inside the house. With a leap, Remo cleared the opening and ran some distance behind the soldiers. Chiun seemed to materialize magically beside him.

They skirted the house silently until they stood behind a lizardy-looking officer Remo recognized as General Elalhassein. The general's hands were clasped behind his back. In the next instant, they hung limply at his sides, his arms having been disconnected at the shoulders. He screamed soundlessly, his eyes rolling, as Remo held him by his neck and whispered, "Where is Randy Nooner?"

The general's mouth opened and closed like a tuna's. "Airport," he managed.

Remo's grip tightened. "More."

"Quat."

"What?"

"He said Quat," Chiun snapped. "I have told you that these persons come from Quat. Why do you persist in asking such irrelevant questions amid this deafening noise?" He stuck two fingers in his ears to muffle the sound of the soldiers' ceaseless gunfire.

"What for?" Remo asked, gripping the general by the eye sockets. His body contorted in pain, his useless arms flailing helplessly each time Remo yanked his head backward.

"To see—to see the sheik," Elalhassein groaned.

"Which sheik?"

"Which sheik," Chiun mocked, pulling his fingers out of his ears. "Remo, your stupidity is unfortunately even greater than your hatred of serenity. I see that as usual I must rectify this matter myself." With a gentle tug, he removed the general from Remo's grasp and tossed him floating into one of the windows of the now-decimated house. Within seconds his body was riddled with the bullets of the Vadassar soldiers, his limbs jerking with their impact, his blood spurting in all directions.

"Silence!" Chiun screeched.

The soldiers stopped at once.

The sudden silence settled upon them caressingly. Chiun's eyelids fluttered, and a smile spread over his face. "Idiot," he said walking away, "there is only one sheik in Quat, and he is of the same name as his father and his father's father and all of the lowly, talkative, meat-eating ancestors before him."

Remo jogged to catch up with him. "Well, if you don't mind, seeing as I don't happen to know every ruler who ever welched on a deal with Sinanju, how about letting me in on the sheik's name?"

"It is inconsequential. Throughout the centuries of their existence, the Quati could never afford the services of a Master of Sinanju. And led as they have always been by the sheik Vadass, they never will."

Remo stopped in his tracks. "The sheik what?"

"Vadass. It is the name of that so-called royal family of camel herders."

Remo remembered the swarthy officers of Fort Vadassar, who spoke their strange language at the press conference, and he recalled the dying words of General Arlington Montgomery: "Vadassar . . . They're going to kill us all." He broke into a run. "Chiun, we've got to get to the airport," he said.

"Where are we going?"

"To Quat. Smitty was right. This army base is about as American as Omar Khayyam. Whoever this Sheik Vadass is, I've got a hunch he's pulling the strings of all these puppet soldiers."

Twelve

The ancient walled palace of Sheik Vadass contained one-thousandth of one percent of the country's population and 99 percent of its income, owing to a longtime national policy of taxation whereby subjects not in some visible stage of starvation were executed as traitors and their holdings confiscated.

The policy was much admired throughout the rest of the developing world. At their annual meeting in the main casino in Monte Carlo, the International Association of Freedom-Loving and Non-Aligned Nations invited the sheik to attend and to address their members on agrarian reform and redistribution of wealth, some of them not yet having figured out a way to get every last coin in their nations. Sheik Vadass did not answer their request. The association passed a resolution calling him a tool of imperialist capitalist Zionism. It ordered a copy of the resolution suitably inscribed and mailed to him, along with a private letter that said they would rescind the resolution if he came and talked to them the next year. He ignored the resolution and the letter. He ignored everything. Nothing came out of Quat. No export. No cash. No natural resources. Not even a breeze.

As Remo and Chiun approached the stone walls on camelback, their guide, a wizened old man dressed in only a loincloth, brought the beasts to a halt.

"We are near the entrance to the Sacred Palace of Vadass," the old man said. "I may go no further, lest I defile the perfect beauty of the palace with my presence. I beg to take my leave here, out of sight of the palace guard."

"I guess they'd grab whatever we paid you for the trip," Remo said.

The old man shrugged. "It is the law of the land."

"I am familiar with your laws," Chiun said. "That is why we are paying you with the contents of our traveling bags. They are filled with food." Chiun pointed toward the camels, laden with heavy lacquered trunks.

The man's face brightened. "All these, sire?"

"All," Chiun said, smiling broadly.

"That's a nice gesture," Remo said.

"All but that red one," Chiun amended, "and the black one."

Remo and the old man unloaded the two trunks for Chiun.

"And the blue one."

"Is this yours, too?" Remo asked, touching a flat yellow box.

"Ah, yes. That is for my sashes. Also the violet."

The camel snorted, having been relieved of all but two cardboard boxes roped together across its back.

"The rest is yours," Chiun said grandly.

126

The old man bowed again. "Many thanks, sire," he said and led the camels away.

"You know, Little Father, it's not exactly easy to sneak into a palace with five steamer trunks," Remo observed.

"Nothing is easy for the slothful."

"You're a real morale booster," Remo said, slinging the largest of the trunks over his shoulder before scaling the wall. He pressed his fingertips into the rough surface and edged upward with his toes, constantly shifting his balance to accommodate the wobbling of the trunk.

"Slow," Chiun said, clucking disapprovingly, "very slow."

"I'm doing my best, Chiun."

"And if a tribe of desert killers were to come running toward you wielding spears, would doing your best prevent them from attacking?"

"If, if, if," Remo said, reaching the top of the wall and sliding silently down the far side with the trunk. "How hypothetical can you get? You're a worrywart, Chiun."

Leaving the trunk on the inside of the wall, he scaled it easily. "If anybody came this way chucking spears at us, then believe me, Little Father, I'd come up with something." He hoisted the second of the large trunks over his shoulder and again began the arduous ascent up the wall.

Chiun smiled. "I am pleased to hear your assurance," he said.

"Why?" Remo asked.

"Because here they come."

From the far end of the wall, a band of small brown men wearing loincloths and turbans and carrying long spears turned the corner and rushed toward Remo and Chiun.

"Oh, hell," Remo said.

"Just do your job. I will distract these hooligans."

As the first of the spears flew toward Remo, who was carrying a trunk across the top of the wall, Chiun jumped high in the air to intercept it with his forearm. With his leg, he kicked another spear harmlessly out of the way. The small brown men came closer, their weapons hurtling through the air. Chiun knocked them away easily, his robes billowing as he leaped to protect Remo from the metal-tipped spears.

"Couldn't we just leave one trunk behind and get into the palace? We could have room service pick it up later."

"Silence, lazy one. When the Master of Sinanju requires your suggestion, he will ask for it." With one hand, Chiun grabbed the last of the flying spears and turned it on the empty-handed warriors. They ran shrieking in the opposite direction.

Chiun poised the spear delicately between his fingers and let it fly with a supersonic crack that filled the air. It entered a brown back, slid through the man's body and continued in its course, impaling two others and depositing the bodies on two others with a bone-crushing thud.

As Remo carried the last of the trunks over the wall, Chiun charged the retreating band. Amid wails and dying moans could be heard the cracking and snapping of bones and joints as the bodies piled up in a formless heap. Within minutes, all that was left of the attackers was a bloody pool in the sand filled with random arms and legs and open, unseeing eyes.

Then, lifting himself lightly off the ground, Chiun adhered himself to the wall and climbed up like a spider. He met Remo on the other side, where the desert had been transformed into lush greenery watered by sprinklers.

"Thank you, Little Father," Remo said.

"Do not worry. I will think of something," Chiun mocked. "Always will he think of something—he whose most recent thought was that he had soiled his diapers. Pah."

"Don't look now, but someone else knows we're here," Remo said. He nodded toward a slight, handsome man swathed in silken jodhpurs and a turban of brilliant white, who strolled casually toward them through the flower garden near the wall. The man stopped well ahead of them and bowed with a flourish.

"Welcome to the sacred Palace of Vadass, gentlemen," he said in precise, softly accented English.

"Yeah," Remo answered. "That was some welcoming committee you sent after us."

The man smiled. "Those were our outer guards. The watchman in the tower felt you were attempting to enter the palace without permission."

"Who, us?" Remo said, watching the man's hands and feet for any sign of quick movement.

"Of course, they were in error. I have been informed by my master that you are quite welcome to the hospitality of the palace."

"Is that so?"

"Indeed, even expected. Please come with me, Mr. Remo. I will have your belongings brought to you." He bowed again and walked with careful steps through the garden. Remo and Chiun followed.

At the end of the garden path, the grounds

opened into vast manicured lawns dotted with sculptured greenery that sported fragrant blossoms in full bloom. In the distance sprawled the Palace of Vadass, its gilt onion domes gleaming in the sunlight.

The man in jodhpurs led Remo and Chiun to a pristine white walkway past a row of uniformed guards. The heavy brass doors of the palace opened as they neared, as if by magic.

Inside, they walked through a huge antechamber of inlaid black and white marble, ornamented by colossal pillars set with glittering colored stones.

"This way," the guide said, leading them to a smaller room where the walls were draped with silk cloth and the floors strewn with fluffy oversized pillows. Since the room had no windows, the glimmer of candles offered the only light. In the corners, cones of incense glowed with smoky fragrance.

"You will please wait here," the guide said. "Refreshment will be brought to you in all possible haste." He bowed again, then stepped quietly through the half-darkness and was gone.

Chiun lowered himself onto a cushion. In a moment, the dreamy silence of the room was punctuated with the sound of bells, high and tinkling.

"What's that?" Remo said.

"Peace be with you," a woman's voice whispered from the darkness. With the same gentle tinkling sound, the girl moved closer, into the candlelight. Remo saw that the bells were on her toes, beneath gossamer harem pants that revealed the inviting outline of her legs. Above, she wore a brief bandeau of bright silk, which covered her breasts modestly while allowing full view of her smooth olive skin. Her eyes were big and almond shaped, rimmed in black to match the dark cascades of hair that streamed to her waist. On her forehead sparkled a blood-red ruby.

"I have brought you tea," she said, her voice husky.

Involuntarily, Remo's nostrils flared to give himself more oxygen. Ordinarily for Remo, one woman was pretty much like another, but for some reason this woman, in this place . . . For the first time in months, he felt a stirring in his loins. He wanted her.

Her eyes never left his as she poured the tea daintily and offered a cup to Chiun. "Would you . . . like . . ." she faltered, gesturing toward the ornate teapot she carried and looking toward Remo.

"I would like," Remo said, touching her hand.

They were interrupted by the opening of the door at the far end of the room. The guide in jodhpurs walked silently into view.

"Mr. Chiun," he said. "Will you follow me, please? Your chambers have been prepared."

"Chiun is sufficient," the old Oriental said. "Of course, 'Awesome Magnificence' would be appropriate."

As the last light disappeared with the closing of the door behind Chiun and the other man, Remo took the beautiful serving girl in his arms and kissed her deeply.

"My body is yours," she whispered, unknotting the scrap of silk binding her breasts. They popped into his hands, round and firm, and her eyes slowly closed as he touched them. "Have me," she said.

Slowly he unwrapped the sash around her waist, allowing her transparent pants to fall to the floor. When she was unclothed, he helped her to undress him until they both stood naked in the flickering

131

candlelight, their eyes locked together in desire. He reached out a hand to caress her, and she brushed her lips across his.

"Beautiful stranger," she said, pulling him onto one of the floor cushions with her. "I was sent to pleasure you, and yet it is I who am pleased."

"We can please each other," Remo said, touching the warm inside of her thigh. Her flesh trembled under his fingertips. With her hands on his back, she pressed him close to her and guided him inside with the movement of her hips.

"Hey, I haven't even gotten to step one," he said.

"Step one?"

"Of the 52 steps—oh, never mind."

And for a suspended moment in time, Remo let himself forget the magical techniques of lovemaking from Sinanju and permitted the beautiful girl in the candlelight to accept him with her body, taking him into her, gasping with his thrusts as he rocked and petted her and brought her moaning to ecstasy and he lost himself in her wetness, her sweet warmth.

She held him tightly. "No man has ever loved me so," she said. Her breath came in ragged gulps. From the corners of her eyes, two glistening tears trickled across her temples.

"What's the matter?" Remo asked gently, pressing his lips to her eyes.

"Go," she rasped, choking on her tears. "Go now."

Remo smiled, bewildered. "Wait a minute. Haven't you ever heard of afterglow? This is where we're supposed to cuddle up and make plans for the future."

"Go quickly, before it is too late," she said, rising to her feet and slipping on her clothes.

"Why?"

"I—" She pushed him away from her. "I have done a terrible thing," she said.

"Tell me," Remo said. "Whatever it is, tell me."

"My master understands that you are an extraordinary man," she began, trying to compose herself. "Difficult to kill. I was sent to weaken you, so that you may be taken. The guards are outside now. Come with me. I will shield you with my body, for I am the sheik's concubine and may not be killed unless Vadass himself orders it."

"Chiun," Remo said, pulling on his clothes. "What about Chiun?"

"The old man has been poisoned. It was the tea. He drank, but you did not. He is dead by now."

Remo swallowed hard. He clenched his jaw as he thought of the frail old Oriental lying poisoned somewhere in the palace, out of Remo's reach. "Where is he?" he demanded, shaking the girl by the shoulders.

"I do not know," she sobbed. "I cannot be forgiven for this. I cannot forgive myself."

Suddenly the door burst open and the light outside the room silhouetted four archers like ghostly shadows, their bows trembling in a wake of arrows shooting blindly across the room.

The girl gasped. Remo saw the arrow enter her chest beneath her throat. With a noise that sickened Remo, she staggered under the impact of the arrow, then fell, blood streaming from her mouth in black strings, darkened by the candlelight.

Remo's attention wavered for a split second when he saw her. It was long enough for another arrow to pierce his right shoulder.

He recoiled with the pain, but it brought him

back to alertness. He forced his mind away from the girl and focused on the hail of arrows, which he fended off easily using only his left arm and his legs. He formulated a plan. Following Chiun's example with the spear warriors outside the palace, he would wait until the archers ran out of arrows, then charge them. He would kill all but one, and would force that one to lead him to Chiun.

But before the arrows were depleted, an eerie crackling electronic noise filled the room, and a woman's voice said, "Stop."

Immediately the bows were still and the archers slipped silently out the door. When it closed behind them, Remo was left again in the shadowy firelit room, which already had begun to smell of death.

There was laughter in the room, familiar laughter, and soon Remo recognized the woman's voice as Randy Nooner's. "All the girls love you, don't they, Remo?" she asked from four different points in the room, her voice amplified painfully.

"The last one betrayed her master for you. That's quite an honor, you know. The sheik's concubine," she sneered. "She was so sure she could protect you, the little ditz."

"Where is Chiun?" Remo demanded.

"Sleeping peacefully. I wouldn't disturb him if I were you. He'll be sleeping for a long, long time."

He squinted through the darkness to locate the loudspeakers, which were hidden behind the sheets of silk on the walls. He blinked, trying to ease a growing pain in his eyes. Even the dim candlelight of the room began to burn with a terrible intensity. And the crackling of the speakers . . . Convulsively, Remo covered his ears to block out the sound.

The movement jolted through his shoulder, reminding him of the arrow wound. It had entered cleanly and gone out the other side—a small wound, insignificant compared with many he had taken—but the pain was worsening fast.

"Uncomfortable, Remo?" Randy's voice crooned. "It's a native poison. Works like strychnine but it's undetectable. No smell, no taste. Sharpens the senses to the breaking point. The old man drank his dose with his afternoon tea. Yours was more direct."

Remo pinched his ears shut to block out some of the booming sound from the loudspeakers.

"This is just the beginning, Remo. It gets worse. Much worse. Listen." Through the crackling of the speakers, Remo heard the amplified shuffling and clanking of gadgets as Randy readied herself. Then his eardrums nearly burst. The ring of a large bell clanged through the room, growing louder with each echo as Randy pumped up the volume on her controls. Remo covered his head with his arms, as if he were protecting himself from falling bombs.

"You should never have looked further than Fort Vadassar," the voice snapped, still shrouded in the echoes of the bell. "You had Artemis. You could have blamed everything on him. That was the point. Instead, you decided to come after me. It was the wrong decision."

"Stop," he cried. "I can't stand the noise."

"Poor Remo. You're so cute when you're vulnerable. Boyish. I like you this way." She laughed again, a high, cruel laugh like a hyena's, which echoed and roared through Remo's ears.

He forced his head up. The sound was deafening, and the light from the candles seared him. When he breathed, the incense in the room nauseated him with acrid smoke.

He struggled to his feet, the room awhirl around him, and looked for a weapon. There was nothing. The pillows, the candles, the incense—everything in the room was soft and pliable. The place was as harmless as a padded cell.

Straining his eyes, he looked at the incense again. The glowing cones were burning in tiny brass lamps. They weighed two ounces at most, but they were shaped in an aerodynamically sound wedge. If he threw them exactly right, weighting his thrust from the middle of his back, at exactly the right angle, he could knock down the loudspeakers and stop Randy Nooner's laughter from pounding in his ears.

His right shoulder was throbbing demonically. He would have to use his left arm. He tried to aim one of the little lamps at the speaker's base, but the speaker was covered with the silk wall draperies, and the poison that the arrow had carried into Remo's body was distorting his vision. The objects in the room appeared to waver and melt together like party-colored spaghetti.

He missed. He stumbled to retrieve the lamp, threw it, and missed again. The effort left him limp and gasping for breath.

Randy's witchy laughter cackled over the speakers again. "The fighter to the end," she said. "It won't do you any good. Your Oriental friend knew that. He didn't struggle at all. He just lay down quietly, the sweet little thing."

"Chiun," Remo whispered. "Hang on, Little Father. I'm coming for you."

It was then that Remo saw the camera. It was poised over the door, hidden in the shadows beneath the drapes of silk. Summoning the small strength he had remaining, he weaved his way across the room and stared up at it.

"You found me," Randy said. "Good. I'd like a closeup of you as you die. The film will make a good conversation opener when I show it at parties." Her laughter reverberated in Remo's brain. "Can you hear me, Remo? I don't think I'm getting my message across. I want you to die."

Her words rang and cracked as the sound became louder.

"I'm turning up the sound, Remo, so that you'll understand me clearly. Die, Remo."

"Die, Remo. Die, Remo," the distorted, disembodied voice echoed.

"Die."

"Die. Die. Die. Die."

Remo felt a small blood vessel in his ear explode. A trickle of blood trailed down his neck.

"I will not die," Remo said.

Slowly he raised his arms toward the camera as if in salute. Then, using his arms as borders, he willed the area between them into focus until he could see the camera clearly. He shifted his weight slightly to center himself directly below it. Randy was talking, but he did not hear her now. Now the universe was a space between his two upheld arms, and nothing more. Only the television camera above him existed. Nothing more. One by one, Remo removed all other sensations from his mind. There were no memories, no past, and no future. Only the camera.

He closed his eyes. The camera was still there, its presence exerting gravity, the only object in Remo's consciousness. He felt it. He was ready.

His knees bent automatically. His back straightened. His heels left the floor, and he was springing reflexively as a cat toward the camera. His hands closed around it. It came away from the wall in a tangle of wires and bolts. It rested in his arms, the weapon he needed.

"You pig!" Randy screamed. But Remo did not open his eyes and pushed the sound out of his ears. He positioned himself in the center of the room and permitted the sound vibrations from the loudspeakers to touch his skin without entering his ears. He felt the corner sources of the speakers, and sent the camera spinning toward one, then another, then another. As the fourth speaker smashed to the ground in a fury of sparks, Remo allowed his concentration to dissipate. The speaker groaned once, then was silent.

Remo sank to the floor.

Thirteen

Quiet.

Remo luxuriated in it. The ringing in his ears stopped. The throbbing from his burst eardrum subsided. His eyes rested on the dim, incense-smoky wall ahead. He pulled his mind back deep into semiconsciousness, away from all thought. There was more in store for him, of that he was sure. There would be plenty of time for worry later. Now he had to rest.

Then the light appeared. It came from nowhere, a blinding expanse of light where the blank wall used to be. It sent him reeling. He blinked and tried to shield his eyes, but the light was unrelenting.

Into it stepped the figure of a man, his shadow attenuated against the yellow-white light. "Come," he said gently. Remo recognized the voice as that of the guide who first escorted him into the palace.

"Where is Chiun?" Remo whispered. ."The old man who was with me?"

"Do not ask, my friend. In the Palace of Vadass, it is always best not to ask." His voice was low and sad.

He helped Remo stand and supported him as he

dragged himself toward the great light. "It hurts my eyes," Remo mumbled, his lips beginning to numb.

"Then do not look," the man said. "Here, to open one's eyes is to look upon pain. One must learn not to see what is too painful to watch."

As they neared the source of the light, Remo noticed fuzzily that the doorway he was walking toward wasn't a doorway at all, but rather the space where the wall once was. The walls must have slid away to form the opening, he thought.

"Where am I going?"

"The royal throne room. The sheik and his woman await you." Remo looked at the man's face. He had remembered it as a handsome face, but now it was creased and careworn. "You were waiting in an adjoining chamber," the man continued. "You and . . . and the dead girl."

"Who was she? I want to know."

"She was not important," the man said bitterly. "Nothing is important here. I must speak with you no more." They walked the last few steps in silence.

The man left Remo when they entered the throne room. Its walls were covered with gold leaf, its brilliance painful. Remo squinted to see. On the gold walls blazed enormous sconces with dozens of candles, and a candelit chandelier 15 feet wide hung from the ceiling, as bright as the sun itself. The furniture was a mishmash of different styles and periods, the pillage of centuries. All but the throne itself, which stood out in Arabic splendor, framed in ornate gold filigree. The occupant of the throne, if there was one, was obscured by thick curtains of many layers of white silk.

Otherwise, the room was empty. It pained Remo to move, but he took a hesitant step forward. As he did, a monstrous pain crashed across his back, and he fell face first to the floor.

"One bows in the presence of royalty, Remo," Randy Nooner said, stepping out from behind him. She was swathed in gossamer veils and held a bronze staff in her hand.

"Chiun," Remo said. "Where's Chiun?"

"You'll see him soon enough. But you're going to answer some questions first. Over there." She prodded him with the staff. He pushed himself to his knees, but a blow across his shoulders knocked him down. "Crawl," she said slowly.

Remo crawled.

Near the throne, Randy sat cross-legged on a Victorian settee. She ripped the veil from her face. "Damn nuisance," she muttered. "I meant the veil, but that applies to you, too. Now, suppose you tell me why you came all the way to Quat, Remo. It's not in the tourist books."

Remo said nothing. Randy raised the bronze staff she carried and slammed it into his wounded shoulder. "Talk," she said.

"Artemis was making those recruits desert for you so that you could have your army. The officers who didn't see things your way on those bases were killed. You did that."

"Ah-ah, Remo. I told you long ago that the recruits were doing the killing. It was the truth. Oh, they had a little encouragement from Samantha's communion brew and Artemis's rhetoric, but the boys took care of their officers on their own. Artemis just gave them a taste of bloodlust with the chaplains they offed at those revival meetings of his. He loved killing, you know. He lived for it. An inspiration to the men."

141

"But he worked for you."

Randy shrugged. "We all work for somebody."

"What about you?" Remo asked groggily.

She smiled. "I suppose it wouldn't hurt for you to know now. You'll be dead before the day is over, even if you run away." She stood up and added, "Which you won't."

She strode over to the throne and pulled a tassled cord hanging down the side of the draped area. The curtains swung apart.

Remo blinked in amazement at the sight. On the middle of the great throne sat a tiny man of indeterminate age, his face as bland as a baby's, his black hair cropped close to his head. In his hands he held a glass ball, which he watched with unending fascination, oblivious to the presence of Remo or Randy Nooner. The man gurgled and cooed as he turned the ball slowly. His face broke into a broad smile, and he kicked his feet playfully into the air.

"Vadass the Sheik," Randy announced sardonically, laughter tumbling out of her.

His attention drawn to her, the baby-faced sheik began to cry until the guide who had brought Remo to the throne room appeared with a new toy to distract him. Without a word, the guide closed the curtains and slipped away.

"That's who I work for. Or what I work for, to be exact. He's got the mind of a cabbage." She cocked her head disgustedly toward the throne. "He's forty-three years old, if you can believe that. But he still needs a woman. That's where I fit in. You're looking at the soon-to-be Queen of Quat, baby."

"Why you?" Remo asked, trying to pull himself from the floor and failing.

"He was neglected, the little dear. His brother

142

was the sheik, and he ran everything. A year ago, the brother went to the trouble of executing all of his male relatives to make sure nobody would try to take over the throne—all but Poopsie here, that is. Nobody thought this drooling fool could take over anything."

"Except you."

She shrugged. "I can't take all the credit. Actually, it was my daddy's idea to have the sheik assassinated and put Poopsie in charge. But he was going to do things the American way, with American advisors and all. It would have given the United States an ally in the Middle East.

"Daddy was going to present his idea to the president, but fortunately he told me about it first. Once I showed him what we could do on our own, Daddy masterminded the rest of the plan. He was the one who picked up on Artemis and found out he was a killer. Daddy figured that a preacher who got off on murdering strangers could do a lot to set up an army, especially if that army had the complete approval of the American people."

"That's what the press conference was for," Remo said. "Artemis brainwashed the recruits at the four army bases for you, then you had them revolt and come to Vadassar."

"That's right," Randy giggled. "Now all those newsmen are telling millions of people that Fort Vadassar is a haven for poor, mistreated soldiers."

"Soldiers for Quat."

"They don't know that yet, of course. Vadassar is on file at the Pentagon as a regulation army base, even though the land belonged to me and Poopsie's money paid for the buildings. It was just a matter of changing records. By the time people find out that the soldiers at Vadassar aren't working for the American government, it'll be too late to do anything about it. My reports say that a thousand recruits a day are deserting their bases and joining the Vadassar forces. Even civilians are enlisting. By next month I'll have a hundred thousand soldiers ready to leap at my command."

"How does Daddy fit in?" Remo asked, sliding imperceptibly away from her.

"Daddy will see to it that Quat gets more financial aid from America than India does. That, or we let loose the Vadassar army on the Texas countryside." She cackled with glee. "Can you see the implications of this!" she said breathlessly. "Never before has a foreign power occupied territory on the continental United States. Quat is going to become a world power. With American funds, we can even build our own atomic arsenal. We'll have Uncle Sam by both balls."

She tapped the brass staff on the palm of her hand. "Now you know." She walked closer to him, her steps deliberate. "This is the end, Remo. What a shame. You were so good in bed."

At her signal, a handful of uniformed guards burst in and rushed toward Remo. Through his blurred vision, they looked like a hundred, stampeding toward him with monkey faces and thousands of arms. They lifted him like a wave.

The poison was working at its peak. Remo's body felt like rubber, his senses chaotic. He was drifting through corridors and stairwells as though he were flying in slow motion, floating past the walls of stone and wood, the footfalls of the men who carried him as loud as thunder.

After what seemed like an eternity of aimless

drifting, Remo's head banged against a cold, hard surface. The movement jarred the numbness from his brain and set it on fire. But he would accept the pain, because to feel pain was to know he was alive. Chiun had taught him that.

Chiun. Through his kaleidoscopic vision, Remo saw him, lying like a statue on the stone floor. He reached out his hand to touch him. The old man was cold.

"Chiun," Remo whispered unbelievingly. He couldn't be dead. He couldn't be.

The anger that rose in him turned to hatred, and the hatred brought him to his feet. The hatred electrified his useless shoulder and forced his arm back and ahead, into the throat of one of the guards, as his left hand exploded into the skull of another. There was no pain, because the hatred was stronger than the pain. He kicked a third guard in the groin, sending him flying in a screaming heap. He held another by the hair as he bashed the guard's head into the stone floor.

Then Remo saw the brass staff swinging prettily through the air an inch from his face, and it was too late. Randy Nooner's face was twisted into an ugly mask, her teeth bared, as she brought the staff down. Remo ducked his head. It was all he could do.

And he thought sadly, as the pain of the blow registered and the blackness began to envelop him, that he had failed. He would never see Chiun again.

Fourteen

He was flying.

It was all so familiar somehow—the rarified air, the tether . . . the tether. Ahead of him, a beast of gigantic dimensions glided gracefully on the wind.

He was back in his dream, the Dream of Death, and the dragon of the dream was carrying him away into eternal blackness.

A monumental force from the West will seek to destroy Shiva, the voice in the dream had told him. But now another voice spoke, high and reedy and absolute in its authority. Chiun's voice.

And it said, *You are that force, Remo.*

Remo stirred in his delerium. "Father," he said.

Silence. He called again. "Father. Father!" he shouted. "Come to me."

I am with you now, the voice said gently. *I am in your mind, where I may help you.*

"How?"

Understand you this. You are Shiva, and only Shiva may destroy Shiva. No harm may come to you but by the wavering of your own will.

"We are poisoned, Father."

Your body can withstand the poison. But it can-

not heal itself without your will. Go into your body and expel the poison from it. Deep within. I will help you, my son.

And Remo felt locking into his mind another force, very strong, very sure. It took him into the depths of his living, physical self, past his weakened muscles, through his organs, diseased by the poison in them. It carried him along the roadway of his bloodstream, cluttered with moving cells and on into the volatile neurons of his nervous system.

This was where the poison had come to rest, among the powerful nerve cells that spurred Remo's senses and reflexes to action. They lay numb and dormant now, their potent electrical charges reduced to fizzling, unconnected sparks. This was where the force brought Remo, and where the voice commanded him to heal himself.

Go within the poison. Eliminate it by your will.

Remo's body shuddered as the strength of Chiun's concentration flowed into his damaged nervous system. He focused on the source of Chiun's thoughts and joined it, and together their combined wills took on an awesome power. Inside the delicate system, translucent ooze seeped out of the sluggish cells into Remo's bloodstream. He gasped as it coursed through his veins, burning like acid. His muscles twitched in spasm from the shock.

The poison entered his heart, and Remo cried aloud with the pain, his unseeing eyes flying open, his fingers clutching empty air.

Father, the pain.

Ahead, the dragon soared to the chilly heights of the stratosphere with Remo following helplessly behind, jerking in agony from the pain.

He was cold. The sky became darker. He was

147

growing numb as the dragon carried him toward oblivion.

Let me go, father. The pain is too great, and I am only a man. Forgive me.

You are not a man. You are Shiva. Withstand the pain and live.

Remo cried out. "Why?" His body racked with sobs. "What's the difference, if you're dead? It's all a joke, Chiun, and I'm tired of laughing. Just let me go."

Things are not as they appear. If I were dead, I would still be with you always. But I live. So must you live also.

"Father," Remo said.

Live, my son.

And the poison passed from Remo's heart and seeped through the layered tissues of his muscles, cramping them in hard knots of pain. Remo bucked forward, vomiting.

Then he began to sweat. Rivulets poured from his skin and dripped into pools beneath his feet. He shook from the cold, the perspiration soaking him in the musty chill of the dungeon.

The dragon turned back. Back into warmth, into light.

Live, my son, the voice repeated.

And he was breathing heavily, and the trembling of his hands subsided.

Remo opened his eyes tentatively. They were filled with sweat, which cascaded from his forehead and blurred his vision. Through the stinging waterfall, he saw Chiun's still form lying lifeless on the cement floor.

His voice was a croak. "Chiun."

148

He had pained to bring the dragon back from peaceful oblivion to live. For nothing.

His shoulders ached. He followed them upward with his eyes to his wrists, which were shackled and strung by chains to the ceiling. His feet dangled free, inches from the floor. He was near enough to Chiun's body to see his face clearly. The old man's expression was peaceful and serene. He had accepted death well.

Remo wept.

Then he thought he saw a movement. Remo blinked twice rapidly to clear his eyes. It was Chiun's face. Something about it had changed.

Remo squinted. Was it his imagination?

No, he decided. There had been a change, an imperceptible change, but enough to alter the utter stillness of the old man's repose.

It happened again. This time, he saw it. "Chiun," Remo shouted.

And it happened once more. By fractions of millimeters, Chiun's eyes were opening. No other part of his body moved. Only the eyelids raised infinitesimally higher until Remo could see the hazel of his irises. Finally, when his eyes were fully open, the old man blinked slowly.

"Chiun," Remo said, the exclamation a mixture of laughter and fear.

The old man didn't respond. "Chiun?" Remo questioned. "Chiun. Answer me, Little Father. Chiun, do you hear me? It's Remo. Chiun!"

The Oriental's lips parted soundlessly.

"Chiun! Say something! It's Remo."

"I know who you are, dogface," Chiun said.

Remo gasped, his joy overwhelming all the pain

149

in his body. "Chiun," he said, almost choking with relief.

"I also know who I am. Therefore, you may cease your incessant wailing of my name, o brainless one."

"I thought you were dead."

"Thinking has never been what you do best, Remo."

Remo looked again at the chains that dangled him helplessly from the ceiling, and blushed with shame.

Chiun floated to his feet swiftly and walked toward Remo, shaking his head and clucking like a disappointed hen. "The worst of it is that this hideous thing was perpetrated on you by Quati, who are possibly the most incompetent warriors on the face of the earth."

He sighed as he inserted a finger between Remo's wrist and the shackle around it and snapped it into fragments. "To be captured at all is embarrassing enough. But to be captured by Quati is unspeakable."

He broke the other shackle, and Remo fell to the floor. "The utter shame of it," Chiun muttered, prodding the wound in Remo's shoulder. He ripped the hem of his robe and bound the cloth expertly around the festering sore. "I will carry this shame with me to my grave."

Remo smiled. "I really thought you were a goner, Chiun."

"As soon I will be. The shame of your capture by Quati will doubtless deliver me into the Void before my time. Let it be on your head."

"Give me all the guilt you want," Remo said brightly. "I'm glad to see you. I was sure—"

"You were sure. You are always sure. And always wrong. Did I not tell you I was alive? Did I not help you—yet again, may I add—to overcome your weakness?"

"I thought that was my imagination."

"Imagination!" Chiun squeaked. "Oh, the odious pride of you. The insufferable arrogance. After overcoming the poison in my own delicate being, I bring myself to the brink of the Void to rescue you from your unbelievable weakness and stupidity, and you call it your imagination."

"I'm sorry, Chiun. I should have known you'd be all right."

"Your imagination is of the same quality as your powers of reason. At best, they are dangerously inadequate. Do us both a service, Remo. Never think. Take up a new profession for which a brain is not necessary. Become a wrestler. Write commercials for television. But do not think."

"I said I was sorry," Remo pouted.

"Sorry, sorry. Sorry us out of here, if you will, Remo. I have seen quite enough of Quat."

"Okay," he said, looking up a stone stairwell leading to a closed metal door. "I'll need your help."

"Of course." Chiun followed him up the stairs.

The door was connected by two giant steel hinges. With his foot, Remo smashed the lower hinge. As the pieces clanked down the steps, Chiun leaped above him to shatter the top hinge. Remo pushed the door outward with the force of an explosion, sending out a wave of smashing steel that reverberated throughout the palace.

"The throne room's that way," Remo said, pointing. "I'll go down this passage, and you take the opposite route."

151

A handful of guards armed with knives and sabers came running down the corridor at them. With one movement, Chiun sent five of them sprawling into the walls, each leaving his own set of indentations. Remo was heading down the long passageway to intercept another group when the whistle of a knife in motion sounded by his ear. Reflexively, he jutted out his elbow, and the knife tumbled to the floor as the guard doubled over clutching his stomach.

He kicked his way through the crowd as the hard clang of steel hitting the marble floor echoed through the walkways. Another saber slashed savagely at Remo's wound, tearing off Chiun's dressing. It immediately began to throb again, but Remo could not let himself give in to the pain. He took the hilt of the saber and wrestled it away from its owner. The guard jumped away, cursing Remo in his strange tongue.

Finally Remo stood at the portals to the throne room. Randy Nooner looked mildly annoyed to see him. She looked up briefly from the magazine she was reading and without expression called, "Guard."

When there was no answer, her lips tightened in impatience. She called again. "I said guard," she snapped. "What do we pay you guys for? Get over here."

No one came.

Remo stalked closer.

"Guard." Hysteria was rising in her voice. "I'll have you all beheaded, you worthless peasants. Hurry up."

Remo neared, his eyes fixed on hers.

"Guard," she screamed.

"They're not coming."

"Help me, you bastards!"

"They're gone," Remo said quietly. "And I'm not. And you're dead."

Randy jumped to her feet and picked up the brass staff she kept nearby. "Don't come any closer," she warned. "I'll kill you."

Remo chuckled. "Try it," he said. "Remember, I'm not poisoned anymore. Miss Nooner, you can throw your little stick to your heart's content."

In a rage, she flung the weapon at Remo. He moved out of the way, and it clinked harmlessly onto the marble floor.

"I guess that's that," Remo said. He came closer.

"Stop," Randy shrieked, the veins in her neck standing out grotesquely, her red hair tangled over her face. She gestured toward the throne covered by white gauze. "Take him," she pleaded. "The idiot. He's the sheik. You can have the country. Kill him and it's yours. Just let me go."

"No thanks," Remo said pleasantly.

Just then, behind the veiled throne, the curtain covering the wall rippled and parted. Standing in the opening was the guide who had first brought Remo to the throne room. His face was stony, and he stood perfectly still beside the throne of the idiot king. In his hands he held a short, thick knife.

"Rajii," Randy called, breathless. "Thank God you're here. Kill him, Rajii. Hurry."

The man did not move, not a finger, not an eyelash.

"Kill him," Randy Nooner ordered.

"The girl killed by the arrows was my daughter," Rajii said in a flat monotone to no one in particular.

Randy growled. "She was a traitor." She gestured

153

toward Remo. "Kill this man or you will be executed," she said hoarsely.

"And you offered the life of my charge, this innocent man with the mind of a tiny child, for your own."

"He's a moron," she spat. "His life is worthless."

"No life is worthless," Rajii said quietly.

Randy sobbed. "Please," she begged. "Please help me, Rajii."

The man nodded. "I will help you in the only way I can," he said, and threw the dagger straight into Randy Nooner's heart.

Her eyes opened wide in astonishment. She raised her hands feebly to remove the knife, but it was imbedded in her chest up to the hilt. As she sank to the floor, Rajii came foward to join Remo before her.

"You ass," she hissed. "He'll kill you, too."

"I know," Rajii said. "May the peace of ages be with you."

Then the sound of death rattled in her throat and she died, her beautiful, cruel eyes blazing with the light from the thousand candles burning in the chandelier above her.

Rajii was the first to speak. "The official documents to the sheikdom are locked in a vault behind the throne," he said. "I will open it for you before you kill me, if you wish."

"Why would you do that?" Remo asked.

"The sheikdom is yours to do with as you like. I ask only that you allow the sheik to live. He is sterile, so there will be no heirs. He cannot harm you in any way. This I beg you. Please grant him his life, for he is innocent of all wrongdoing in this terrible place. Grant me this one request, and I will prepare

154

all the documents to declare you regent and official heir. Then you may dispose of me as you will."

Neither of them noticed Chiun move silently beside them. "Who are you?" Chiun asked.

"Only a servant," Rajii said.

"You do not have the bearing of a servant. I ask you again. Who are you?"

The man paused, clenching his jaw, then he spoke. "My name is Rajii Zel Imir Adassi," he said. "The name belonged to one of the wealthiest families of the region. Then Vadass—the sheik's brother —took over the throne and executed everyone who could usurp his power, including the males of all the noble families, and confiscated the fortunes of these families. Mine was among them."

"Then why didn't he kill you?"

Rajii's head hung in shame. "Vadass disliked me particularly because I would not permit him to take my daughter for his sport." He spoke so quietly that his words were nearly inaudible.

"My wife died when she was very young, and I never remarried. My daughter, Jola, was all I had. I treasured her. I wanted to save her for a man who would treasure her as I did."

Remo saw Rajii's hands tremble, and was filled with sadness for the broken man. "So when Vadass began his purge, he first took my daughter to be his concubine, his toy. . . ." He bit his lip and tried to compose himself. "And then, as a prank, he took me as his servant so that I might watch her in her degradation. He said that my job would be to serve his feeble-minded brother, to be reminded always that even this Vadass was master to me.

"But, in believing that every man's heart was as small as his own, Sheik Vadass made a great error.

155

For my daughter was still alive, and because of that, I counted myself a lucky man. And the boy became an even greater joy, because with him and his simple ways, I was needed. He will never grow and understand like other men, but he has my love."

"Did Randy Nooner know any of this?"

"No. They didn't care. When the Americans came—the woman and her father—I knew that the end was near. They took everything by force. They were even worse than Vadass. At least the sheik never used his poor brother, as the American woman did."

He sighed deeply. "I knew that one day we would all die in a bloody coup. That day is come. Jola is dead. But the sheik need not die. He has harmed no one, and never will. Please," he said. "My life is no longer of use to me. I give it to you willingly. But I will remember you in all my prayers through all eternity if you will grant my charge his life."

Chiun unfolded his hands from within the sleeves of his kimono. "Show us the documents," he said.

Rajii nodded, defeated, and led them past the throne, where the sheik made happy gurgling sounds inside his curtained domain. Behind the wall draperies stood a large metal vault with a combination lock, next to a broadcasting hookup with a television monitor. It was from here that Randy had observed and tortured Remo with the deafening sound from the loudspeakers. Rajii opened the vault and pulled out several yellowed parchment documents sealed in wax and tied with red ribbons.

"Herein rests the official line of succession," Rajii said as he unraveled the scrolls on a low table beside the vault. "The American woman and her father never saw these. They could never have had a legal claim to the throne. I will amend these to make you the rulers of Quat." He picked up a quill and dipped it in ink.

"Halt," Chiun said.

"But it will be official. I have the seals."

"I trust that it will be official," Chiun said. "But we do not wish to be rulers. That is not our place in this life."

Rajii looked, bewildered, from Chiun to Remo. "I do not understand."

"Affix your own name to the documents, and we will witness. You will be regent. You will find a wife and marry and bear children who will become your heirs. And you will pass on to your children your wisdom and loyalty, so that the people of your land need never again starve or suffer for the whim of their sovereign."

"I . . ." Rajii said, astounded. "Surely, I cannot—"

"You will," Chiun commanded. "It is the only way. Quat has been a plaything for incompetents long enough. You can try. That is all we ask. If you fail . . ." He shrugged. "Quat has been failing for centuries."

"I don't think Rajii will fail, Little Father."

"Perhaps not," Chiun said. "He who possesses a heart will always find hope to fill it." He smiled kindly and bowed to Rajii.

Rajii returned the bow. "May I ask you a question, sire?"

"You may."

"It is the same one you asked of me. Who are you?"

"I am the Master of Sinanju, and this fellow is my . . . as you say of your sheik, Remo is my charge."

The sheik belched in the background. "I really appreciate the comparison," Remo said.

"I have read of you in the legends of other lands," Rajii said respectfully.

"Quat has never been worthy of the services of my ancestors before. But perhaps you will rule differently. If so, and you find your domain in need, you have my permission to call upon my services."

"Thank you," Rajii said. "I am deeply honored."

"For free," Remo added. "Oof." He caressed the spot on his ribs where Chiun's elbow had attacked like a viper in the night.

"For a reasonable fee," Chiun corrected.

Fifteen

Senator Osgood Nooner was having a nightmare.

It had to be a nightmare, because sensations such as the pain he was feeling just didn't happen in real life.

There he was, the People's Senator, tucked away in the safety of his bed, feeling his skull being crushed to powder by a thin young man with thick wrists who looked disturbingly familiar.

He knew it had to be a dream because when he opened his mouth to scream, no sound came out. It was a classic indication.

Then he realized that he wasn't screaming because the underwear he had tossed on the rug for the maid to pick up in the morning had been stuffed into his mouth.

"Hi," the stranger said.

Nooner tried to place the face, but couldn't.

"The reporter at the Vadassar press conference," Remo reminded him.

The senator's rounded eyes glimmered with recognition.

"Well, I just wanted you to stop worrying about

159

us nosy reporters. I'm not going to print a thing about you."

Nooner nodded, trying to seem appropriately grateful.

"See, Senator, I'm not really a reporter at all."

The senator's eyebrows arched inquiringly.

"I'm an assassin."

Slowly Nooner's eyes closed, and he thought he was going to faint.

"Do you know why I'm here?"

The senator gulped, swallowing some cotton lint and a loose string.

"I want you to write a letter."

A whinny of relief sounded from Nooner's nose. He nodded enthusiastically, eager to demonstrate his willingness to write whatever craziness the stranger had in mind. One phone call to the president in the morning, and everything would be straightened out, possibly with this nut behind bars.

Remo held fast to the senator's head while he rummaged in the nightstand with the other. "Now, here's a paper and pen," he said patiently, as though he were talking to a small child. "You just write what I tell you, okay?"

Effusive nodding.

"Okay. Address this to the director of the CIA."

For a moment, the senator shot Remo a glance from the corner of his eye, but a new pain in his head brought his attention riveting back to the page. He wrote down the director's name and address.

"Very good," Remo said. "Now you write down that all the Pentagon files on Fort Vadassar are false, and that you were responsible for tampering with the records. That ought to be good for a couple of years in the pokey, don't you think?"

The senator's pen hesitated in the air.

"That is, unless you'd rather be murdered right here and now by me. I think I've already told you that's my profession."

Nooner wrote vividly of the replaced files.

"Now put down that the property Fort Vadassar is on belongs to your daughter, who's been in on the whole scheme from the beginning."

With a shrug, the senator did as he was told.

"And that you hired Artemis Thwill to drug the troops at those army bases and have the chaplains killed."

Senator Nooner banged his fist on the nightstand and shook his head adamantly. Soon a sensation having the same effect as the sound made by a razorblade on a chalkboard streaked down the side of his face.

He wrote.

"Let's see," Remo said. "What else?" He drummed his fingers on the top of Nooner's shining bald head.

Finally free of Remo's grip, the senator whirled around and yanked the stuffing out of his mouth. He opened it to call for help. Suddenly Remo's fingers grazed the senator's throat, and Nooner uttered a sound like the tail end of a scratchy record.

"Help," the senator wheezed.

"Whazzat?"

"What the hell do you want from me?" Nooner asked, his voice a passable impersonation of Marlon Brando playing the Godfather.

"I want a confession, Nooner, so that the blame for this fiasco falls where it belongs." Remo smiled, pleased with his eloquence. "Sit down," he ordered.

When Nooner sat, Remo pinched a cluster of

161

nerves on his neck, which paralyzed every muscle in the senator's body except for those of his writing arm. "Okay," Remo said. "So far you've tallied up ninety-nine years or so. How about including the Quat story—how you had Vadass assassinated, how you planned to marry off your daughter to the retarded sheik, how you imported the commanding officers at Fort Vadassar from Quat. Hey, I'll bet they're illegal aliens, too. Senator, you're going up the river for a long time."

The senator's whole right arm trembled, but he wrote down the information.

"Now, for the grand finale, let the CIA in on your plans to control the United States with your zombie deserter army. And don't forget to mention that you engineered the massacres at those four army bases to get your recruits. That ought to wow 'em out in Langley."

Nooner wrote until the final period was placed near the bottom of the page.

Remo released him. "Is that all?" the senator asked.

"Put down that you swear the above to be true and verifiable, then sign your name. I saw that in a movie once. It made everything legal or something."

"All right." He signed his name with a flourish. "What are you going to do to me?"

Remo folded the paper and placed it in an envelope. "Got a stamp?"

The senator pointed at a desk. Remo placed the stamp on the envelope, addressed and sealed it, and put it in his pocket. "I'll mail it, just to be sure," he said with a wink. "To answer your question, I don't know. I was planning to kill you, you know, but you've been so cooperative and everything. Besides, sending you to jail for three hundred years or so might be more interesting. If you're dead, nobody will care much whether you were guilty or not."

The two men sat staring at each other for what seemed to both of them like a long time. "Tell you what I'm going to do," Remo said, slapping his thigh. "You call the director of the CIA at home right now and tell him everything in the letter, and I won't kill you."

"How do I know I can trust you to keep your word?" the senator asked.

Remo smiled. "You don't. Now you know how your constituents feel."

Wearily the senator picked up the telephone and dialed. He greeted the sleepy voice at the other end of the line with a monotonal rendition of the contents of his letter.

"Whaaat?" the CIA director said, yawning. "What kind of crap is this?"

"Tell him that if he doesn't send a team to pick you up within five minutes, you're going to blow up his house," Remo whispered.

Nooner gave him a disgusted look and parroted the words back into the phone.

"Well, okay, Ozzie, if that's the way you feel about it. I'll get a car over there right away. You just hang loose, okay? Okay?"

"Sure," Nooner said, and hung up. "Satisfied?"

Remo nodded. "And just in case you think you can get away with saying you were forced to lie under duress, the president is personally going to order an investigation of you in the morning. You've left tracks, Senator, and this letter points to the trail. Bye bye."

He waved and placed one leg outside the window.

163

"I'll hunt you down," the senator threatened. "You'll be exposed for the crackpot you are. I'll be cleared in a minute."

Remo slapped his forehead. "Oh yeah. There's one thing I forgot to tell you. Just slipped my mind, I guess."

"What's that?"

"I don't exist," Remo said, and slithered down the face of the building minutes before the CIA car arrived.

Sixteen

It was high noon on the parade grounds at Fort Vadassar. Chiun grumbled and complained all the way up the barbed-wire fence.

"Is Emperor Smith never satisfied?"

"We just have this one last little job to do, Little Father, and we're done with the assignment." Remo paused at the top of the fence to get an overview of the base. "After this mess, I'd say we were entitled to a couple of weeks of R and R in the sun. The tropics, maybe. Jamaica, or Martinique—"

"Or Sinanju," Chiun said dreamily. "The sun shines nicely in Sinanju."

Remo cleared his throat. "Maybe Smitty'll put us on another case."

"What else remains to be done here? We have eliminated the false priestlet. We have eliminated the red-haired woman. We have eliminated the senator. What is left?"

"We have to eliminate this army," Remo said grimly, watching Fort Vadassar's 100,000 recruits in drill formation. "They deserted in herds after the press conference."

"But you said the newspapers would retract their statements today."

"That's not going to stop these zombies," Remo said. "They've been brainwashed. Anybody who tries to disband this army is asking for war."

He looked out over the parade grounds. The number of soldiers had swelled to fill the base, and all their faces bore the blank, burned-out stamp of Randy Nooner's control. Each platoon on the grounds was at least 8,000 men strong and led by top Quati officers, their telltale sabers dangling from their belts.

Remo shook his head as the officers shouted their commands. Each of the thousands of men in each platoon obeyed in perfect robot precision.

"Tahiti. If we get through this, we deserve no less than Tahiti."

"Sinanju," Chiun insisted.

"We'll talk about it later." Remo let go of the barbed wire and dropped to the ground. "Let's start in the officers' mess. It's lunchtime."

The officers' dining room hardly qualified as a mess hall. Silken draperies adorned the walls, and ornate filigreed brass outlined both entrances. Candles lit the room, their flickering light seemingly in rhythm with the droning ancient music in the background. The hearty laughter of men rang out over the babble of Quati spoken at the tables. On a small stage, a rotund woman in harem costume gyrated seductively. Other women similarly clad made the rounds of the tables, offering drinks and honeyed desserts.

Spotting Remo and Chiun in the doorway, two of the officers rose and asked them to state their business. Remo stuck a finger through one man's left temple. "That's my business," he said. Chiun dispatched the other officer with a swift kick to the crotch, causing the man's legs to part near his navel.

In an instant, the place was in an uproar. The woman hid, screaming shrilly. The men rushed toward Remo and Chiun, their sabers bared.

One by one they fell, their swords flailing wildly in the air. Remo and Chiun worked a double inside line attack, systematically knocking down the crowd of officers as though they were dominoes. When they had completed the inside line near the far entrance, they doubled back in an outside line, obliterating the rest.

"Your elbow was bent," Chiun snapped.

"Save it, Little Father. We've got too much work to do."

"It is important. Without a straight arm, it is possible to maim without killing. That is both cruel to your target and dangerous to you."

Remo was abashed. "I'll remember next time, Chiun," he said. "There's no time to check the bodies now. We've got to get to the parade grounds before someone shows up here."

"Very, very dangerous," Chiun said, visibly angry. They left through the back entrance.

Beneath the rubble of broken bodies, a hand moved slightly. It pushed to remove the weight of five men piled on top of it, but could not. The hand snaked slowly between the bodies as the owner of the hand gasped and panted for breath. Then the hand shot out past the topmost corpse, a little flag signaling the life Remo's faulty elbow had spared.

The man pulled and writhed his way past the grisly load bearing down on him. He was in great

167

pain. Nearly all his ribs were broken. Occasionally his lungs would fill up, and he coughed and spat blood. He was dying.

Still, he wrestled with the remains of his fellow officers, trying not to look at their bizarre positions and blank stares.

For the first time in his life, he missed Quat.

An eternity beneath the bodies. Then air. The man passed out for seconds at a time. But between the blackouts, he crawled.

He crawled to the door and scratched at it like a dog until it opened from his feeble efforts. He crawled outside, where he could still see the small outlines of the two strange men, the American and the old Oriental, who had come from nowhere to kill the Quati at Fort Vadassar. They were heading for the parade grounds. They wanted the rest of the officers. They were professional killers, of that he was sure. But the younger one had been sloppy with him. He had made a mistake, a tiny mistake, a fraction of an inch, but enough to spare the officer's life for a few minutes. He would use those minutes now to see that the assassins paid for their mistake.

He crawled to a small building the size of an outhouse and fumbled in his pocket for a key. Vomiting blood, the officer placed the key in the door and turned it. The door opened to a narrow stairway.

He wouldn't be able to crawl down the steps. He wouldn't last long enough. So he held his breath and propelled himself forward, bouncing down the wooden stairs like a withered, bleeding beachball. If he lived for five more minutes, the strangers would be dead. Five more minutes.

* * *

"They'll listen to anybody," Remo said. "If we knock out one unit at a time, I think we can control them without a lot of casualties." He looked at his watch. "Smitty said he'd have troops here in twenty minutes. If the officers are gone by then, the recruits ought to go peacefully."

"Where will Emperor Smith send a hundred thousand men?"

"Who knows. But he wants them deprogrammed, not dead. We take out only the officers, right, Chiun?" Remo asked apprehensively.

"He is a very generous emperor, but none too intelligent, I fear. A hundred thousand enemy soldiers may not take to captivity with docility."

"The country will be up in arms if we kill the recruits," Remo said, trying to sound persuasive. "It's not really their fault they're in this place. They got suckered into it. They are Americans, after all."

"No one forced them to come here," Chiun said drily.

"Look, Smitty says don't kill the recruits. That's the assignment, like it or not."

Chiun shrugged. "It is obvious that the emperor is quite mad," he said. "But a contract is a contract."

The officer blacked out at the foot of the steps. He spat, but his lungs were weakening fast, and he couldn't remove all the blood that was building up in his throat. He was strangling.

An inch at a time he wormed toward a square on the wall. The entire building had been constructed around the contents of that square, and the officer would reach it. It would be his final act of vengeance against the two intruders.

169

At the base of the wall, he curled his fingers and edged them up the wall. He had lost his sense of pain. He felt as if he were inside a vacuum as his blood streamed down the front of his shirt. He hated the American stranger now more than ever. He hated him for killing his countrymen, but more than that, he hated him for the wound he carried, which was so painful that it was beyond pain. It would have been better by far to have died with the rest.

The square. He had reached it. With a bitter smile, the officer stuck a fingernail into the edge of the square, and the small door opened easily. They would die now, the intruders.

With his last trembling effort, the officer pulled the red lever inside the square on the wall, and the wail of 40 sirens screamed in alarm throughout the base.

Overhead, the stampeding of a thousand feet thundered out of the barracks. On the parade grounds, the officers looked about them, their weapons drawn. Remo and Chiun stood in the midst of an army of well-trained, well-armed soldiers, who turned to face them, one platoon at a time, in eerie synchronization, as the first of their commanders shouted the order: "Kill."

The officer at the alarm switch let his hand fall heavily to the floor. With the last of his breath, he laughed.

"Kill." The command seemed to echo from flank to flank.

"Kill."

"Kill."

"Kill."

Moving as a unit, the blank-faced soldiers raised their M-16's to shoulder level.

"Halt!" Remo said confidently. In an aside to Chiun, he whispered, "I told you, they listen to anybody."

A bullet whizzed past Remo's head.

"Hey, what happened? You guys are supposed to stop."

The commander of the platoon sneered. "Now they listen only to us," he said. "My apologies." He raised his right arm. "Fire!" he called.

Chiun leaped into the middle of the nearest platoon, his long robes billowing. Remo followed. He didn't know what Chiun was doing, but this was no time to ask questions.

The old man was running through the platoon at nerve-shattering speed in a strange elliptical spiral pattern. As Remo followed in his wake, the soldiers in the platoon lost aim and turned, confused, upon one another, each blank stare confronting another expressionless face, their rifles clanking together as Chiun wound the formation of recruits into a dense, ever-tightening mass.

"Not *with* me," Chiun hissed. "Opposite. Reflect me. The ellipse within the ellipse."

What in the hell is that, Remo wondered, although he obeyed unhesitatingly. He swerved into a curve exactly mirroring Chiun's movements, creating along with him a complex, orbiting double helix within the flank of soldiers. When the platoon was crushed into a chaotic group of men struggling to move like fish in a net, a strange thing happened. The mass began to move.

Suddenly Remo saw the impenetrable logic of

Chiun's words: *The ellipse within the ellipse.* For slowly, with each orbit Remo and Chiun made in opposite directions, they were moving the bewildered soldiers toward another platoon without ever exposing themselves to bullets outside the cramped mass of recruits. Inexorably, the platoon meshed, amoebalike, into the next, creating a rampaging confusion that made it impossible for the soldiers to fire.

"Kill them," a Quati officer screamed as he was spun helplessly into the teeming fray. Chiun made a tour near the officer and flicked a fingernail at his chest. The officer dropped. When the growing mass of recruits moved in its perfect ellipse toward the third platoon, the officer remained, trampled, on the spot where he fell.

The mass grew to cover nearly two acres, a beehive of restless, pulsating activity, as Remo and Chiun pushed the mindless unit toward another, their weapons at the ready.

They were on the verge of absorbing the fourth platoon when the commanding officer, a colonel, shouted an order and the platoon scattered to form a circle around the huge, bumbling entity Remo and Chiun had created.

"Fire!" the colonel commanded. The soldiers surrounding the group fired randomly into the mass. The recruits on the periphery dropped instantly.

"They're killing their own men to get to us," Remo yelled. But Chiun did not respond. Instead, Remo noticed a change in the pattern. On Chiun's side, the unit bulged and receded like a bubble, absorbing each soldier within firing range one at a time. Remo repeated the pattern on his side, keeping the mass tight while he formed the tentacles that reached out to pull the soldiers on the outside into it.

There were two platoons left. As Remo moved, he saw the two commanding officers signal one another, and the platoons turned to face one another.

At a second command, they marched resolutely together, forming one large unit that came at the beehive group of four captured platoons in a slow, deliberate offensive.

"They're going to sacrifice all of them, Chiun," Remo panted as he made what seemed like his ten-thousandth round inside the group. He was tiring, and running on reserve.

"Take one of the officers," Chiun said, passing by in a flurry of motion.

Remo looked at Chiun's back unbelievingly.

The two platoons had marched into firing range, and the front line was kneeling. The rain of bullets began.

"Are you kidding?" Remo yelled. "There's nothing between us and them but a million units of ammo."

"Go," Chiun said, his thin voice straining. "I will hold the formation. But I cannot move it forward alone. And I am growing weary."

A sliver of alarm streaked up Remo's spine. If he himself was bone-tired, Chiun would be exhausted. The Korean had passed the 80-year mark long before, and holding the formation meant traveling in double-time. Even before Remo left the group, Chiun's pace had quickened to a speed that made him nearly impossible to see.

Swallowing hard, Remo darted out of the mass and into the smoky field dotted with flying bullets. As he did, the two platoons 500 feet in the distance shifted their target from the unwieldy, stagnant group of soldiers held by the old Oriental to the single man in a black T-shirt, armed only with his hands. Remo saw the barrels of 16,000 M-16's more slowly toward him with terrifying accuracy.

Almost immediately a bullet grazed Remo's thigh. It helped. Inside his body, he felt his adrenalin pump to overload level, and he needed that for the pattern he would use.

Chiun had taught him the pattern—if it could be called a pattern at all—long ago, but he had never had to use it in actual combat before. It was an extension of the movement that allowed him to dodge a single bullet fired at him from point-blank range, a quick shifting of balance entirely without rhythm.

Chiun had explained that the exercise was difficult because in all of nature, as in all of the training of Sinanju, rhythm played a crucial role in the scheme of survival.

Rhythm and balance. Without them, chaos, and nature would not abide chaos for long—not in the planets, nor in the human organism. Chaotic gene patterns created mutants that died early and could not reproduce. Rhythm and balance were everything. Remo's breathing was rhythm. Chiun's formation around his mass of recruits was rhythm. The bullets that were fired at Remo resulted from pure, mechanical rhythm with the triggers that fired them. It was as though each molecule ever created, as Chiun had once explained, had made a pact with nature before its existence not to disturb the rhythm of the universe.

But the secret of avoiding bullets was antirhythm, balance without rhythm, movement so fast and formless that it defied rhythm without throwing the balance of the body into chaos and the inevitable outcome of chaos, self-destruction.

Avoiding one bullet was easy. The loss of rhythm and the amazing speed required for it lasted only a fraction of a second. The damage wreaked on Remo's body was no greater than that inflicted by an insect bite. But to dodge—how many bullets? A million? Two million? He would have to create a pattern of anti-rhythm at perhaps 100 times the speed of a champion Olympic sprinter.

Remo appeared to be moving slowly and in a blur. It was easy for the soldiers to get a bead on the young T-shirted man but, inexplicably, impossible to hit him.

"Fire," the officers commanded.

"Fools, kill him!" Both officers took out their pistols and emptied their barrels at the weird, slow-moving target with fuzzy outlines. As he moved closer, one commander rubbed his eyes. The other squeezed his shut and shook his head. Neither could believe what he was seeing, for the young man appeared to have no face.

He was within ten feet of the front line, and still they could not hit him. At eight feet, one of the commanders reached an inescapable conclusion and related it shakily to the other: the man was unkillable.

"He is of the undead," the officer said, his voice heavy with dread.

"There are legends in Quat. . . ." the other replied slowly.

At five feet, the two of them ran screaming for cover.

Remo was losing his focus from the strain of the anti-rhythm pattern, but the two figures were large enough to tackle without perfect vision. Not waiting to regain his rhythm, he sprang on one foot toward the two officers, spiraling in the air like a football. He fell on them both, killed one immediately, and held the other in front of him by the collar.

"No," the man quavered. "My God, my merciful God—"

"Tell them," Remo whispered, his speech thick and slurred from the ordeal he had put his body through. As he spoke, the rifles of the two platoons turned automatically on Remo and the officer he held squirming in front of him.

"Hold your fire!" the commander screamed. "In the name of all that is sacred on this earth, hold your fire!"

"Tell them not to try to harm us," Remo said. "Under any circumstances. And make them get rid of their rifles." He felt his eyes rolling back into his head.

"Maneuvers completed," the officer shouted. "Destroy your weapons. Repeat. Destroy your weapons."

In the distance, Chiun's group vibrated to a halt. The old man staggered outside the group, holding a hand to his forehead.

The sound of splintering rifles filled the air for minutes, then stillness settled over the parade grounds. The only noise was the whimpering of the Quati officer dangling in Remo's hands. Remo wound his hand slowly around the officer's neck and strangled him. Ahead, the troops observed the scene with faces as impassive as statues.

Remo dropped the man and walked over to Chiun, who had replaced his hands inside the

176

sleeves of his robe. "Are you all right, Little Father?" he asked.

"Yes," Chiun said, nodding. "Are you?"

He was dizzy. He was nauseated. He was cold. And the wound in his shoulder from the Quati archers still hurt. "Yes," Remo said, just before he fainted.

Seventeen

Remo came to at the sound of approaching tanks. "Here comes the cavalry, just after we need them," he said groggily.

"It is a trademark of all armies to be only in places where they are not wanted," Chiun said.

The tanks burst through the barbed-wire fence as if it were made of cobwebs, and ringed the parade grounds, trapping the recruits inside their circle. After the tanks came over 100 closed vans to remove the recruits from Fort Vadassar. The men entered the vans without resistance.

"I wonder if they will ever behave as normal men," Chiun said.

Remo shrugged. "Randy Nooner said something about 'Samantha's brew.' They're probably drugged. A couple of days in isolation, and it ought to wear off."

"Get moving," a voice from behind them said. Remo turned to see a burly American sergeant prodding recruits into a nearby van. "Hey, youse guys too. Get in here."

"Suck wind," Remo advised the sergeant.

178

"Leave those two alone," a one-star general ordered from a jeep moving toward them.

"Yes, sir," the sergeant said, snapping in salute.

The general's driver brought the jeep to a halt and scrambled out. "They fit the description, sir," he said.

The general rose. "Gentlemen, I've been instructed personally by the president to escort you to your destination," he said.

"And where's that?"

The general paused as a film of red rose from his neck to his cheeks. "To the No-Tell Motel," he said with as much dignity as he could muster.

"Smitty," Remo muttered under his breath. "Always looking for the cheapest rates."

Remo and Chiun climbed into the jeep. It rumbled past the convoy of tanks and vans to a rundown string of cabins 15 miles away, where they were dropped off with a salute from the general.

There was a reservation for them in cabin 5 of the No-Tell. The woman at the desk got the key for Remo. "Oh, just a second, there's a message for you, too," she said, unfolding a piece of paper stuck in the slot for cabin 5. "It says call Aunt Mildred."

"Great," Remo said disgustedly, taking the key from her. He let Chiun in the dingy room and slammed the door. "What a hole," he said.

He picked up the phone and dialed the number that would route the call through on a safe line to Folcroft Sanitarium. Smith picked up the phone on the first ring.

"What do you want now?" Remo said.

"I'm glad you're alive."

"No thanks to you. Setting us against an army is

179

your idea of fair play, I suppose. Not to mention holing us up in this rat's nest."

"The motel room was only so you could make this call," Smith said. "There was no point in wasting money on fancy accommodations just for a phone call."

"Suppose we'd like to rest. We almost got killed out there, you know."

"I'd rather you didn't," Smith said flatly. "The general the president sent for you knows your whereabouts."

"So what?"

"It doesn't hurt to be cautious."

"Why bother? You're going to see to it that the guy gets transferred to some obscure combat unit out in the Indian Ocean anyway."

There was a pause on the other end of the phone. "That was unnecessary, Remo," Smith said finally.

"But true."

Smith cleared his throat. "You'll be pleased to know that the investigation of Senator Nooner began today," he said, changing the subject. "It seems he got the Assistant to the Chief Clerk of Records at the Pentagon to switch the Vadassar files around, and then had the man killed. It's all coming out in the wash. The senator is going to face at least five hundred counts of murder. The case will make history."

"Happy as a clam, aren't you?" Remo said.

"And Samantha Thwill is in custody in Texas on accessory charges. The army convoy picked up samples of everything in the kitchen at Vadassar, and if any of that stuff is drugged—as it probably is—the finger will point to her."

"Well, friend, my finger is pointing in a different

180

direction," Remo said testily. "What you did to us was unjust and unfair."

"Somebody had to do it," Smith said. "Just get back here, and I'll see to it that you and Chiun get the vacation you deserve."

Remo's mouth dropped. "You mean it, Smitty? How'd you know? As a matter of fact, a vacation is exactly what we had in mind. Tahiti, I think. Tahiti would be great. You have the tickets ready, and we'll be there in four hours."

"I've already arranged for passage—"

"Aw, Smitty," Remo said, grinning, "you're really too much. I underestimated you. You're a prince. Chiun, we're on our way."

"—to Sinanju," Smith finished.

"What?"

"Chiun's been asking me for months. I thought it would be a treat for the both of you."

Remo turned from the phone to stare beady darts at Chiun. The old Oriental smiled sweetly and nodded. "The sun shines nicely in Sinanju," Chiun said.

"Thanks, Smitty," Remo said. He decided not to kick a hole in the wall. "Remind me to bring you a souvenir from the glorious shores of Sinanju. Like maybe a poisonous snake. And I hope this case puts you up to your pecker in paperwork."

He hung up with a clatter and yanked the telephone cord out of the wall.

"Are we on our way to Emperor Smith?" Chiun asked, his feet bouncing in a little dance of joy.

Remo pulled down the shade to the nicotine-colored window. In the darkness, he kicked off his shoes and plopped onto one of the room's two sagging beds. A puff of dust rose from the blankets. "We're staying here," he said. "Forever. I'm never leaving this room. We'll probably come down with some filthy disease and die here, and it'll serve Smitty right. Sinanju. I'll bet you two were in on this all along."

Chiun continued to dip and swirl in the darkened room, his thin voice chanting a happy Western melody:

> Disco Lady
> Won't you be my baby . . .

CELEBRATING 10 YEARS IN PRINT
AND OVER 20 MILLION COPIES SOLD!